About the Author

Birte Hosken was born in Germany in 1965. Having met her future husband during an exchange visit to Penzance she moved to Cornwall in 1989. Her fascination with the beauty and mystique of the Cornish coast and countryside has inspired her to take her passion for writing further. *Petroc's Church* is her first book.

Dedication

I dedicate this book to my husband Des and my two children Julia and Jason.

Birte Hosken

PETROC'S CHURCH

AUSTIN MACAULEY
PUBLISHERS LTD.

A CIP catalogue record for this title is available from the British Library.

ISBN 9781786122506 (Paperback)
ISBN 9781786122513 (Hardback)
ISBN 9781786122520 (E-Book)

www.austinmacauley.com

First Published (2016)
Austin Macauley Publishers Ltd.
25 Canada Square
Canary Wharf
London
E14 5LQ

Acknowledgments

It has taken not only time but also a certain amount of courage to finally get *Petroc's Church* published. I have been passionate about writing from very early childhood. A reminder of how young I was when I first put pen to paper were my small, home-made books that we found when clearing out my mother's house in Germany. Moving my mum to Cornwall in 2014 meant that a lot of this early work had to be looked at but then it had to be destroyed. Although it brought a big smile to my face I did not consider it worthy of keeping.

For years I intended taking my love for writing further but family commitments, other interests and moving house always came first. Once the children had grown up and we settled in Carbis Bay near St Ives I resolved to "go for it". I was thrilled to think that Austin Macauley were prepared to publish Petroc's Church and I thank them for it.

My thanks must also go to my friend Olli Crocker, a fellow tennis player at Penzance Tennis Club, whose painting of Godrevy Lighthouse caught my eye and consequently provided the cover image for my first book.

I recognise it from the first bar. That piece of weird music, unconventional, heavy, unusual and definitely disharmonic. Nobody has ever written songs quite like that and nobody would have a recording of them unless they had been at one of the very few live concerts that the band has given. "Monopoly", although up and coming, rarely perform in public. I have seen them here in Cornwall last summer, at a beach bar in Perranporth to be precise. It was on one of those crazy nights out with Tina. At the time she was madly in love with sexy Andrew Whitehead, a cool lifeguard in his spare time and a PE teacher by day. He was the guitarist in a small local band and we were travelling all over the place to be near him. If it had not been for Andrew we would never have seen or heard Monopoly. Tina had had too much to drink and... best to leave it at that.

I am still trying to establish where the sound is coming from. At this time of morning, the start of a glorious day, there are already plenty of cars in the car park. Carefully I venture forward, keeping an eye on the small wooden hut that serves as my shelter and office, to scan the colourful sea of cars. Clutching my bag with the change I try to listen. Does it come from the shiny silver Mercedes with the personalised number plate? Or the old white banger that surely has not passed its last MOT? What about the green metallic sports car that has seen better days? A cloud of dust announces the arrival of a new customer.

"I thought the car park was free at this time of day!" I hear a voice shout behind me.

Like lightning I turn around.

"Oh, Jake, you scared me then!" I reply and smile.

The driver of the super cool and just as super noisy VW camper van reaches out of the window to shake my hand.

"When I saw Don looking after the car park yesterday I thought you wouldn't be coming this year," Jake explains.

He and his now heavily pregnant wife Lauren are running the beach shop and café at the other end of the large car park in summer. In low season Jake usually helps his parents who have a popular hotel and restaurant in St Ives.

"This is my first day," I tell him. I notice that Monopoly have gone quiet.

"Anyway, great to see you back!" Jake says and drives off towards his workplace. Before I can even blink a small queue has built up behind the bright orange VW and I have to take money and tell people where to park.

For the last three years I have come to Cornwall each summer. My grandparents own this massive field near one of the most spectacular surfing beaches in Hayle, and it is a real gold mine during the summer months. An old family friend who has only recently retired from an office job is playing cashier for most of the time but when the summer holidays start I am his boss and I am earning good money. On a day like today the car park can be full by 11 am. The worst are the days when business is slow – two cars all day because the surf isn't right, its overcast, too windy, raining or simply too cold. I've seen it all during the last three seasons – and it's not only the boredom factor. At times you have to fear for your life, no, honestly, I've had to put up with some pretty bad abuse as well. How dare we charge for car parking? I've heard every single swear word in the book, definitely too rude to repeat. Talk about road and car park rage! I've had people fighting over the best spots or what they think are the best spaces. I've seen all sorts. Drivers accidentally scratching brand new treasures, surfboards sliding off vehicles, wetsuits too tight to get on or off, kids with splinters in their feet, grannies red as lobsters with sunburn, local VIPs expecting special treatment, you name it.

I could write a book – "The life of a car park attendant" or something similar. Would make interesting reading, I bet! What I haven't seen though, in all those weeks I've been here, is a drop-dead gorgeous man. I am serious. That kind of thing does obviously not use Grandad's field. I've seen some stunning cars around here but no drivers to match. There's someone at home in London who I fancy but he would never dream of coming to Cornwall. He is, well, out of my league, I suppose.

Yet another Ford Fiesta has just arrived. The elderly man behind the steering wheel is shaking his head.

"Don't you think £5 a day is a bit steep? I remember paying only £3 last year," he says to me.

"It's been a fiver for the last couple of years, sir," I respond politely.

What looks like his wife beside him moans.

"Sometimes I don't know why we bother going to the beach, Fred. It is by far too hot today," she says.

I put on my professional smile.

"There are still some spaces in the shade over there. If you park next to that Toyota," I explain and point to the dusty white car near the dunes that separate Grandad's field from the wide beach.

Without further ado Fred hands me a five-pound note and drives off.

I love this job. No, not really, but it's better than pulling pints in a dingy pub or cleaning toilets in hotels – that's what my best friend Lolita is doing this summer anyway. I am out here in the fresh air, I am my own boss and I am having, well, yes, fun. Smiling to myself I enter my little hut. My Gran never fails to provide me with plenty of food and drink when I leave each morning. As there is nobody arriving at the moment I pick up my mobile and text Lolita. Almost instantly I receive a reply from London.

"It's raining here and I've made five beds already. You won't believe the mess people leave in their rooms and the loos..." I read. Poor Lolly.

I've tried to persuade her to visit me in Cornwall this summer, just for a week, but she needs the cash, that's the trouble. Lolly is saving up for a trip to Australia. Her boyfriend is down under on a one-year student exchange and she is desperate to see him. To be honest, I am not really sure if she's not wasting her time and money though. Paul has got a bit of a reputation...

"You don't charge for motorbikes, do yah?" I hear a voice outside the hut. I see nothing but black leather and a fire red helmet. Behind the visor a couple of heavenly blue eyes look at me intently.

"Yes, I am afraid so," I reply, getting a flimsy green ticket ready. Strict instructions from Grandad – motorbikes £2. Obviously, I don't say it quite like that but I point at the hand-painted board that is attached to my hut.

"Two pounds please," I say confidently.

14

"Forget it. I'll park the bike over there," Blue Eyes responds.

"As you wish but you will earn yourself a hefty fine if the warden comes along," I remind Black Leather Man.

"And does he turn up here often?" he wants to know.

"Daily!" I reply, although that is not absolutely true. The patrol van goes past two or three times a week – at the most – but I have to look after my business.

Begrudgingly Blue Eyes pulls a couple of quid out of his tight leather trousers.

"Here you go, you win," he says. Revving up the engine both motorbike and rider shoot forward. I don't even get a chance to see Black Leather Man taking his gear off as the next customer arrives. It can be so easy – middle of the road Vauxhall, couple of beach babes, simply handing over the money and off they go! No problem – why can't they all be like that?

No time to dwell on that subject. Here comes smiley-face Ian from the surf school. Ian is my big brother, no, not really, but it feels like that. He's only a couple of years older than me, blond, super fit and never short of girlfriends. Trouble is I fancy dark-haired ones, "tall, dark and handsome" as they say. I like Ian a lot but not that much, if you know what I mean.

"Hi, great to see you!" he greets me enthusiastically. He's looking fantastic as usual. Is it surprising that the girls are queuing up for him? Tina absolutely adored him until she got this crush on Andrew Whitehead. Admittedly he's the same type, just older and according to Tina much sexier.

"Hi, Ian," I say and give him a shy little kiss.

"How are you doing?" I enquire.

"Could be better. I twisted my ankle yesterday and it hurts," Ian admits.

It's always a pleasure looking at his well-trained legs but his right ankle looks distinctly swollen.

"Have you seen a doctor?" I ask him immediately.

"Yep. Went to casualty straight away and had an X-ray. The girl I was teaching is a nurse. She insisted," he answers smiling.

"I'm off to see Jake. Did your Grandad tell you that Lauren is going to have a boy?" he wants to know.

I shake my head.

"Well, apparently so and he is due any day now," Ian tells me, limping on.

Behind Ian three cars are queuing up.

"See you later on the beach," I shout after him and try to concentrate on my job.

The day passes very pleasantly. Don arrives late afternoon to take over so that I can enjoy a couple of hours on the beach. As the car park is nearly full there is not too much for him to do but Don just likes reading a book and having a break from his demanding wife Joyce who always finds jobs for him to do around the house.

Delighted to be free on this beautiful sunny afternoon I rush down the high dunes towards the surf school. The sea looks calm which is great for me but not for the surfers. All I want is a swim. I am looking for Ian but can't find him. Disappointedly I change into my swimming costume. There is nobody on the beach I recognise. No doubt Tina is spending the day at Perranporth where Andrew Whitehead is on duty. I have suggested to her that she should get herself into trouble with her surfboard and make Andrew rescue her but she is too embarrassed to try it. When she was after Ian she was hanging around the surf school all day every day which was better for me. As I approach the water's edge I realise that I am missing her. She is a good friend really, although I only see her in the summer. I think the only way I can lure her into visiting me in London is if Andrew's band were having a gig up there but that is most unlikely. Just as unlikely as Monopoly playing at Wembley stadium. In my mind I can't get rid of that strangely catchy song I have heard in the car park earlier on.

The salty seawater is up to my knees now and it's absolutely freezing. In the distance I spot Ian. He is lying, pretending to sunbathe, on a surfboard. Seconds later a dark creature appears from under the water. The glistening black body belongs to a girl − no surprise there − dressed in a wetsuit and she is trying hard to push Ian off. I am up to my waist in the sea, just about, and shivering. Yes, I do have a wetsuit at my grandparents' house but I did not bring it. I thought the water would be lovely on such a nice day.

Suddenly, and I am being really brave as the cold water touches my tummy, I have this melody in my head again. There is nothing quite like Monopoly and I will never know which car the music came from.

Eventually I get used to the icy water and have my swim. Ian has introduced me to his latest girlfriend, number hundred and something, but soon it is time for me to return to my grandparents' home. The last time I came to visit the house next door was empty but tonight I spot a car in the drive and the "for sale" sign has gone too.

"You didn't tell me that *Seabreeze* has been sold!" I put my Grandad on the spot.

"They've only arrived today. Jacob down at the pub told me that a couple from up-country have bought it," Grandad says. He's standing by the window looking for movement next door.

"As a holiday home?" I enquire.

"Jacob didn't say but he thinks they are of retirement age so maybe they have come here to stay for good," Grandad replies.

Gran is out in the garden, her favourite place. I catch her peering over the hedge and trust Gran – she's made friends with "next door" already.

From the bathroom window I watch her talking to a lady and I mean a lady. The new neighbour is beautifully dressed. She is wearing an elegant pencil skirt and a silky blouse, her grey hair tied up loosely. If she wasn't of retirement age, as Grandad calls it, I would almost describe her as sexy. I am like glued to the window. Gran is laughing. I can hear her from here and I can see next door smiling too. Then Mr Next Door appears in the garden. Wow! He's even better! He's in a suit, well-built, short grey hair, a bit old for me, of course, but just like my dream man would look like when he is around 60. I watch him put his well-tanned hand on his wife's slim shoulder and he is smiling at Gran who is almost lying on top of the hedge now so that she can talk to them. Suddenly I hear Gran's voice shout.

"Richard, Richard, please come here and meet Max and Louisa!"

Grandad obediently marches down the garden path. He shakes hands with the new neighbours across the gate. I am still at the window wondering what Max will make of Grandad's rugged shorts and worn-out trainers. Gran does not look brilliant tonight either. She is in her gardening gear consisting of washed out jeans and a grubby polo shirt which shows off her not so great figure. There is not a gram of fat on Louisa. She is really pretty for an elderly lady. Max has gone into his new home but he soon returns with a bottle under his arm and some glasses. I am looking forward to spying a little longer but just then I hear my Gran call my name. Oh dear – my hair is still wet and full of salt. I've got my oldest T-shirt on and flip-flops. Panic-stricken I grab my brush but I must not let the gathered party wait.

"Please, Jen, meet Max and Louisa!" Gran says.

I am totally in awe of Max. He is certainly attractive. My heart skips a beat when he passes me a glass and fills it with champagne. Yes, I mean proper champagne, the really expensive stuff. Louisa is very nice too. I am OK with her but her husband is something else. I like everything about him – his looks, his voice, his smile. He tells us that he was in business in South Africa and they've lived out there for many years. I fiddle nervously with my wet and dirty hair – and then the phone rings, no, not Grandad's but a mobile in Max and Louisa's new home. Max hands the bottle with the last drop of champagne to Grandad and rushes inside.

"He'll take some time to get used to retirement," Louisa comments. Minutes later she collects the empty glasses and joins her husband in the house.

Gran is putting her gardening equipment away. I follow Grandad back inside.

"He's going to be trouble, I feel it in my bones," he says to me.

"Why do you think that? He seems very nice to me," I say quickly.

"Bit of a snob. Champagne and all. He definitely thinks he's something special, he has got a big car…" Grandad replies, turning his eyes up heavenwards like only he can do.

I smile mildly. "He can't help looking good and being successful," I whisper, but I don't think Grandad has heard me and I am glad about that.

I don't normally have a lie-in in the mornings but Don has got something on tonight so he rang up last evening to change his shift. He is going to do his stint from 7:30 am to 2 pm and I am going to take over then. When I look at my alarm clock it is almost 10 o'clock. Although it is cloudy this morning it is still quite warm. I've had the window open all night. Stretching and yawning I get up. I can hear voices outside. Surely Gran is not talking to the new neighbours again across the hedge?

Carefully I approach the window. My room is overlooking the back garden and I can also see some of Max and Louisa's garden which is naturally in a sorry state considering how long *Seabreeze* has been on the market. My desire to see Max worries me slightly but I lean out of the window to get a better view of next door. Heaven help me! There is another Max in the garden but much, much younger! Old Max is showing young Max around. I am staggered. Young Max isn't that young, mind. I would guess he's about 25. I watch as mother Louisa is joining her men. She is looking different today; she's in trousers and a tight-fitting polo shirt, very classy. Old Max wears blue jeans and young Max black ones. Both father and son look smashing. If Tina thinks that Andrew Whitehead is the sexiest man around then he has just been beaten. Young Max is my type, from head to toe. I keep watching. Old Max is pointing at some shrubs, pacing up and down the weedy lawn when suddenly young Max makes a strange movement, right in the middle of the grass.

You don't need to be an expert to recognise what that is – and here it is again. How silly! Pretending to hit a golf ball! Don't you realise that you are being watched? I can't take my eyes off it though. After the umpteenth swing into nothing but good Cornish air I have to agree with my grandad. That young Max is definitely a real show-off. The neighbours' garden is not even big enough for crazy golf. If someone of his physique was going to hit a golf ball from next door's garden it would fly as far as the sea. Oh, good Lord – just as I decide to go to the bathroom the show continues. Young Max is exercising, obviously totally oblivious to my watchful eye.

"Lance, Petroc is here!" I hear a female voice shouting.

It's Louisa's posh voice, no doubt about it. Young Max, no, Lance, stops showing off his fantastic body and rushes to the front of the house. Shame, I can't watch him there. Disappointedly I finally go to the bathroom.

I am trying hard to forget Lance whilst I am having my breakfast but the picture of him in his parents' garden occupies my mind. For the minute I don't want anyone to know that I have been spying.

"Do Max and Louisa have any children?" I ask my grandad who is reading the newspaper.

"They didn't say," Gran replies on his behalf. I am about to tell my grandparents what I've seen from my window but then I resist. All I want is to meet Lance and I am already scheming how to go about it.

My thoughts are interrupted by the ringtone of my mobile phone.

"Tina!" I exclaim.

"Hi, are you down at the car park?" she asks me.

"Not at the moment. I am going to be down there from 2 pm," I reply, walking towards my grandparents' lounge.

"No doubt you are at Perranporth," I say to Tina.

"Yes, but I want to see you," she responds.

"How's Andrew?" I enquire, although I am not really interested.

"He's OK. Jen, there are a couple of boys I want you to meet," Tina tells me. I am about to say that there are a couple of boys next door that I want her to meet too but, of course, I don't say that, considering I have not even met them myself yet.

"We'll meet you down at the beach at 7 pm and we'll bring a few drinks," Tina says.

Do I detect that Andrew Whitehead is not in favour anymore?

"Okay, I'll see you at 7 pm then," I tell Tina.

That is the end of the conversation. I am now standing at my grandparents' front window, hoping to be able to look into *Seabreeze*'s drive but Gran's high bushes make any views impossible. It is time to tell Grandad of my plans for this evening so I go and search for him in the garden.

The sun has decided to come out after all and Grandad suggests that we have lunch at Jacob's pub down the road. I think that that is a very good idea. Perhaps I will get a chance to talk to the landlord about Max and Louisa. Gran is surprised that I am "dressing up" for lunch but I just ignore her. I have known Jacob and his wife Mary for many years and I don't normally bother to get changed to go to their pub. The small beer garden is a real suntrap and always extremely popular with visitors. Tina used to help out during the summer months but since she has been travelling to go to the beach at Perranporth she's packed it in. Deep inside I am hoping to bump into Lance but there is no sign of him or his family members.

Jacob serves Grandad with his favourite ale and stops at our table for a chat.

"Have you met your new neighbours yet?" he suddenly asks. My ears prick up.

"Oh, yes!" says Grandad, turning up his eyes just like last night. Jacob is interested to hear what the newcomers are like.

"Looks like they've got a bit of money to spend then," the landlord deducts dryly.

Grandad nods.

"I can see that I am going to fall out with them sooner or later," he remarks.

I can't understand why Max has made such a negative impression on him but I keep quiet. Gran has her eyes closed and is enjoying the sunshine. I don't think she's too worried about next door at all.

I am almost late for my shift. Don is busy selling tickets and directing cars when I arrive.

"I've had a couple of youngsters who didn't want to pay this morning," he reports as I am taking the money bag off him.

Secretly I am hoping that said youngsters were not Lance and Petroc whoever he may be but, of course, Don would not know. I send him on his way and take a seat in my shady hut. My mind is on Lance when a minibus full of girls arrives.

"We are looking for the surf school car park," the driver says.

"I'm afraid they don't have a separate car park. The surf school is right here," I advise, pointing towards the glistening sea.

I have a feeling that this group is going to play up but they negotiate peacefully and get away with a standard £5 ticket. Normally we charge buses with a higher rate but the car park is not going to be full today so I succumb. Everyone is happy.

In the distance I can see Jake rushing around his café which is absolutely packed. We are all working hard to satisfy our customers.

It is almost 6 pm when Tina arrives. She has a new car, well, it's new to her but it's actually quite old. In the backseat I spot two young men – surfer dudes, no doubt. Tina stops the Peugeot in the middle of the entrance to my car park, jumps out and embraces me. She has put on weight. Her white T-shirt is stretching tightly over her voluminous breasts.

"Great to see you. Please meet Jack and Tristan," she says, knocking onto the back window of her car. The two lads wave reluctantly. I wave back but I am not really interested in them.

"We'll set up camp along the beach somewhere. Please join us as soon as you can," Tina demands and hops back into the car.

"I've invited some more people along – so don't be late," she adds as she drives off.

I have to say that I don't fancy a party on the beach tonight but when Tina is determined to do something she does it – unless it involves Andrew Whitehead. She turns abnormally shy then.

At 6:30 pm I start packing up. If anyone arrives now they don't need to pay anymore. A lot of locals know this. They often come in batches of five or ten at this time of day. I lock the creaking door of my wooden hut and take the money over to Jake. He gets his staff to count it with the shop and café takings, then banks the lot on his way home. So far nobody has ever mixed the bags up but I am always afraid that one day Jake will employ someone dishonest and the whole system will break down. Grandad seems to be happy with the arrangements. It certainly suits me tonight.

I eat the rest of my sandwiches before going down to the beach at 7 pm. On the horizon the sun is beginning to set beautifully, not surprising that there are still quite a few people walking along the shore. Although I have come here many times in summer since my early childhood I still have to stop in my tracks to take in and admire the fantastic scenery. The natural, unspoilt beauty of what I call "our beach" is just amazing. On the eastern side of the bay I can clearly see the rugged rock that is home to Godrevy Lighthouse with its stunning white, octagonal tower. Right behind me the high, rocky coastline stretches along the vast expanse of sand. The evening sun gives everything a golden, magical colour. As I walk towards the spot where Tina and her friends are I listen to the powerful but somehow calming sound of the waves rolling onto the pebbliest part of the beach.

Ian and his girlfriend Annette have been invited last minute. I can see them heading towards a large circle of young people. Everyone is seated in the sand, only Tina is standing up like a school teacher and doing a head count.

"Anyone missing?" I ask her carefully as I approach.

"Yeah, loads couldn't make it but we won't worry about it," she replies casually.

Her two new boyfriends are distributing the drinks. My eyes are scanning Tina's old blanket that she has spread out on the warm pebbles at the upper end of the beach. She has brought a ghetto blaster and CDs. Having planted his can of coke into the sand Tristan is sorting through the large pile of plastic disks. He discards one after the other but I pick up my favourite. It's the copy of Monopoly's CD that we bought after the concert last year.

"Who listens to rubbish like this?" Jack asks the gathering. He is now holding up a handful of CDs from Andrew's little known band.

"I like them," Tina defends the attack on her musical taste.

"She likes Andrew, more like it," one of the invited girls says laughing.

"Oh dear. He was my teacher last year," another girl pops up. Tina looks at me helplessly.

"Anyone for Monopoly?" I ask in order to change the subject.

"If we must..." the boys give in. I bend down to load the disk.

"They will be performing live in Newquay on Saturday," Ian's girlfriend suddenly announces.

I turn the volume up.

"Anyone going to that?" I enquire, looking at Tina. She seems undecided. Somehow she has changed since last year. I sit down and watch Ian. He has one arm around his girlfriend and a bottle of cold beer in the other hand.

"How's London?" Tina asks after a while.

"It's fine, thanks," I reply a little formally. For just a split second I am reminded of my daily life in the city.

"Any decent men?" she wants to know.

"Yes, some," I respond, not smiling. My fingers are nervously fiddling with the empty Monopoly case. All of a sudden I grab the multi-coloured cover tighter. I have never looked at the picture on the case properly.

"Lead singer Petroc Hayman," I read. "Is that a common name in this area?" I say to no one in particular.

"What?" Tina asks.

"Petroc," I reply.

"Well, not really. Why? Do you know someone called Petroc?" she asks curiously.

"No, I just wondered," I answer quickly.

Tina smiles.

"Petroc was a Cornish saint, I think. Do you like that name?" she enquires. I shrug my shoulders and I am instantly reminded of Lance. What's that short for? Lancelot? Just the thought makes me smile. Slowly I put the case down. Monopoly are getting on my nerves but I make no attempt to turn the music down.

Ian and Annette don't stay too long but the rest of us are having a fun evening. Tina is in her element. She is flirting with Jack and Tristan at the same time. Unfortunately the girl I was having an interesting conversation with decides to leave fairly early so I feel a bit out of it.

By the time most of the people have moved off the beach it is getting dark and with the tide turning the evening breeze feels increasingly chilly. Everyone is pulling on their sweaters. Both Tristan and Jack are fed up with Tina's advances. They are hitching a lift with a couple of other boys who are going back to Penzance. Although I am freezing I am glad to be left alone with Tina. The cool summer wind is getting stronger as we tidy up the beach before walking back towards her car.

"So what's happened to Andrew?" I finally ask her.

"He's engaged," Tina says sadly. She is almost in tears, her head bowed. I put my cold arm around her.

"You did not seriously think that he was ever going to be interested in you, did you?" I ask daringly. Tina gives me a venomous look.

"I'll never get over him, never," she confirms.

"Are you going to come to Newquay with me on Saturday then?" I continue, trying to get her out of her depressed mood. Tina's dull expression changes into a wry smile.

"There is something that you are not telling me, Jen. Why that sudden interest in Monopoly?" She digs her car keys out of the deep pocket of her tight shorts.

The car park is virtually empty now. In the dark I count three cars, excluding Tina's.

There are no cars in *Seabreeze*'s drive at all when I return home. Max, Louisa and their show-off son must be out somewhere. Admittedly, I am disappointed but it is late and I need to go to bed.

"I'm going to go to Newquay with Tina on Saturday night," I announce at breakfast. My grandparents do not look particularly happy about it but fortunately they do not try to stop me. Without any further discussion about my plans I leave the house early to start my shift on the beach. It's going to be 7:30am to 2:30 pm today. Despite the lovely red sky last evening today's weather is pretty dull so it could well be a very long, boring day for me.

Usually, when I arrive at the car park in the mornings there are no vehicles parked in the field as Jake's security guard puts a barrier up when he makes his final round of inspections late at night. Only very few people have a key for the padlock. This morning there is one old red car left in the car park and I am wondering why. Getting my keys ready to unlock I pull my mobile phone out. I have to talk to Jake.

"I'm off to the hospital. Lauren has gone into labour," he reports nervously.

"Did your man lock up last night?" I ask quickly.

"Yes, of course, well, I think so – why?" Jake responds.

"There is a car left in the car park," I say.

"Sorry, I can't sort that out right now. Just give them a ticket and see who picks it up. I've got other things to worry about at the moment," is Jake's hasty reply.

"OK, yes, I understand, I'm sorry. Good luck anyway," I say and ring off.

It is surprisingly cold this morning. What has happened to the mild Cornish summer that is being advertised in all the holiday brochures? The wind is whistling noisily around my wooden hut. Shivering I retreat to the little bench inside and write a short message to the driver of the left-behind car asking him or her to pay me £5 when they return. Determined to claim my money I pull my thick sweater on. Then I make my way over to the old red banger to put the note behind the windscreen wipers.

Leaving my hut unattended in the car park for a moment is a risk but I dare to walk slowly up the short path through the dunes. Sheets of fine sand are being blown across the shoreline by the fierce westerly wind. My eyes are scanning the almost deserted beach. On the horizon I can see someone running.

"Early morning exercise," I say to myself, thinking of Lance.

"Early morning..." before my wild fantasies play any further tricks on me I return to the car park in order to take another good look at the old Fiesta. An untidy pile of CDs is lying on the passenger seat. My heart begins to beat a little faster – not only one but three are saying *Monopoly* on the front. I step back from the car as if it is threatening to blow up in front of me in the next two minutes.

Totally intrigued I return to my small hut and with that the first drops of rain are starting to fall. It will take only a couple of seconds before my hand-written message is going to be washed away. Quickly I put my old baseball cap on and make a note of the car's registration number.

"I'm going to get you," I whisper.

A couple of dog walkers pass the car park and proceed along the road but so far I have not seen anyone else going to the beach or leaving it.

Jake's staff have arrived late to open the shop and café but there are no customers. The sky remains grey with soft rain falling steadily. Grandad rings me on my mobile, asking me to close the car park early.

"The forecast is not good, Jen. You may as well come home until 2 pm and then we will see about Don," he suggests kindly. As much as I am hoping to catch the overnight parker I cannot refuse to go home now.

By 10 am I have returned to my grandparents' house. In this weather the neighbours will not be in the garden so it is going to be a thoroughly tedious day. I ring Tina to see what she is up to.

"Not a lot," she tells me. I wish I could talk to her about the mysterious red car but I decide not to.

"If you are not working this afternoon you could come over to my place," Tina invites me.

I am grateful for the offer. Gran has gone to Penzance for a doctor's appointment and Grandad is at the pub helping Jacob with his monthly bar stocktake. Having finished my phone call I feel lonely. Like a thief I venture outside to see if Max's large Mercedes is back. It is and there is also a works van from an electrical company parked in the drive. Seems like they are doing a job at *Seabreeze*. The rain has become quite heavy since I've returned from the car park. It is nothing but a terribly miserable day.

I spend most of it at Tina's house in the centre of nearby Hayle.

"It's dry now," I tell her cheerily, looking out onto the busy road in the middle of the afternoon.

"Let's go for a drive in your new car," I suggest rather selfishly.

"Good idea. Where are we going?" Tina agrees, picking up the car keys from her desk.

"I must find out about Jake's baby. Why don't we drive down to the beach café and see if they've got any news?" I propose.

"Okay fine," says Tina and off we go.

Having made this short trip so many times before I don't take much notice of the traffic on the bumpy access road to Grandad's field but I am determined to look out for the old red car. As soon as we arrive in the car park I can see that it has gone. Obviously, I am disappointed but not surprised. We park right in front of the café. Most of the staff have been sent home. Only a few of the locals are sitting around a large table with a bottle of bubbly. "It's a boy!" they shout as we enter the otherwise almost empty restaurant area. Tina and I smile happily.

"Six pounds and a quarter ounce – mother and son are doing fine," one of the remaining waiters announces proudly.

"What's he called?" Tina wants to know.

"Trevellyan Jake," one of the female kitchen staff informs us.

"How lovely – sounds like a proper Cornish name," says Tina.

Just like Petroc, I think but I say nothing. Lancelot, Merlin, King Arthur and the Knights of the Round Table... all kinds of strange thoughts go through my mind but I remain silent. Tina has already organised two glasses for us so that we can join the party.

"You are Jen from the car park, aren't you?" a young waitress suddenly says to me.

"Yes," I reply carefully.

"There was a chap here earlier who was looking for you. He said he owed you a fiver," she says and hands me the cash.

"He said he was sorry," the waitress adds.

I look at Tina, Tina looks at me.

"Did he say who he was?" I ask eagerly.

"No, no idea. He wore sunglasses and a woolly hat – in this weather. I don't know…" the waitress reports and turns away.

I hold the five pound note in my hand, almost caressing it now. Tina laughs.

"Uh, you never know. You may have missed the chance of a life-time there" she teases.

Shrugging my shoulders I pull out a piece of paper from my jeans' pocket.

"Well, at least I've got the registration number!" I announce triumphantly.

The unsettled weather continues until Saturday. I've hardly been down to the beach. Tina and I have gone shopping in Truro, visited some of her friends, spent time with Jacob at the pub, gone over to Camborne to see Jake, Lauren and the baby and nothing is happening next door, apart from the noise the builders make. Grandad is trying to be understanding but at times he has to turn the TV up to full volume because of the drilling that's going on.

It's Saturday morning and Gran is outside talking to the postman. From the lounge window I can see Louisa turning into her drive. She stops the car where Gran is standing, obviously apologising for the racket they are making over there. It's only at the last minute that I spot that there is someone in the passenger seat of the Merc but I can't tell if it's Max or Lance. When Gran gets in I cannot hold back any longer.

"Who was that next to Louisa in the car?" I ask straight out.

"Her son. He's got a strange name," Gran says.

"Lance," it slips off my lips.

"Yes, something like that. How do you know that?" Gran enquires.

I have no option but to tell her what I have seen and heard in the garden a few days ago.

"Like the look of him, do you?" Gran asks smiling. I nod. Yes, I feel really embarrassed now. Gran shakes her head.

"Too posh for you, dear," she says and walks off to the kitchen.

Well, the truth hurts, doesn't it? I am sure that Lance is far too posh for me but I fancy him or at least

I think I do. Quietly I follow Gran. She looks me deep into the eyes and comes up with an ingenious idea.

"I am going to bake a cake. It's no sweat putting two into the oven. Perhaps you'd like to deliver one next door later on? I know Richard does not agree but I think we owe them something in return for that champagne the other night."

It's unbelievable – I have never waited so desperately for a cake to bake in all my life. Gran's cakes are absolutely superb. Nobody can bake cakes like she can – next door will be impressed. Impatiently I go up to my room so that I can start getting ready for tonight. Tina is going to pick me up at 7 pm. She has already worked out where to go before attending the gig. I am not really keen on Newquay on a Saturday night but it can't be worse than some of the places I go to in London. Newquay is the most notorious Cornish party town. It can get a bit hairy there late at night. Hopefully Tina will see sense and take me home early should matters get out of hand. Pacing up and down in front of the mirror I pull my mobile phone out of my jeans. Tina has just sent a message: *Ian and Annette coming as well. Pick-up Ian's house at 7.15 pm. See you later. Tina.*

I look at the text, considering a response. It would certainly save Tina a trip if we all met at Ian's house. He lives just outside of Hayle. I feel sure that Grandad will drop me over. My fingers are trembling as I type my short reply. I am so nervous. Gran's cake must be almost ready. In front of the mirror I rehearse what I will say when I go next door.

Half an hour later Gran hands me one of her famous masterpieces.

"Tell them they'll only need to shout if they want any help at any time," she says with a twinkle in her eye.

She can see how excited I am. Balancing the cake carefully on a plate – great idea to use a china plate that they will have to return, Gran – I step out of my grandparents' front door. Nervously I walk up the new neighbours' path. Everything at *Seabreeze* has been turned upside down and inside out since the builders have started to work here during the week. Holding the cake in one hand I use the other to knock firmly on the door. I can hear movement inside the house.

"Lance? There's someone at the door. Can you answer it, please?" I hear Louisa's friendly voice inside.

"Oh, yes, please, Lance. Please answer the door," I whisper, my heart beating like a drum.

"It's alright, darling. I am on my way," I hear Max say and with that he opens the heavy front door. The disappointment is written all over my face. I am making a proper fool of myself, all stuttering and shaking. Max takes the cake out of my hands. His attractive smile calms me down a little.

"That's very kind of your grandmother. Many thanks. This cake looks delicious," he says politely.

He does not ask me in. The old hall of the once so grand house is just a building site now and very dusty.

"I'm sorry we are in such a mess here. We are going to have a housewarming party later in the year. Please tell your grandparents that they are invited," Max says, depositing the plate with the cake on the bare floor boards.

I am trying my hardest to stay at the door a little longer, just in case Lance appears from somewhere.

My grandmother asked me to tell you…" I start quickly when suddenly I am interrupted by the noise of a nail being hammered into a wall.

"Sorry about that. Lance, can you stop that for a minute, please?" Max shouts up the stairwell but the hammering continues.

"Anyway, if ever you need anything…" I start again.

"Thanks, thank you very much," Max replies before I can finish my sentence, and with that he basically sends me on my way. I smile sadly in defeat and return home.

So that is that – total failure, if you ask me. Posh Lance is either disobedient or has bad ears – or both. I am beginning to think that he is a complete idiot – time to concentrate on getting ready for Newquay.

Grandad drives me to Ian's house. It always feels like coming home when I go there. As usual Ian's little sister Annie is happy to see me. She says that she is keen on visiting me in London, obviously she is not so little anymore.

"Why don't you come up at the end of October during the school holidays?" I ask her kindly.

Annette and Ian, sitting in the cluttered front room, are indulging in alcoholic drinks already. It's only 7:15 pm but it is Saturday night so what can you say? Tina arrives late which is nothing unusual. I am having a strong Cornish cider to kick off with. Not being used to drinking too much alcohol I can soon feel the effects of the ever so tasty but potent local favourite.

We eventually leave Ian's place at 8:15 pm. Why does Tina have to drive so fast? Ian and Annette seem to enjoy the journey, all cuddled up on the backseat but I am frightened to death.

"Are we in a rush?" I ask her eventually and she slows down a bit.

Still, we reach Newquay in what seems next to no time whereas finding a parking space, suitable for Tina's poor manoeuvring skills, is another matter.

Ian knows all the surfing beaches in Newquay and around. He is also an expert on the coolest evening venues. All the pubs and bars in the area are absolutely packed on a Saturday night in the summer. It's like being in a different world over here.

"Monopoly are a lot more popular than they were last year," Annette tells me.

I have a feeling that she is a bit of a fan.

Tina seems fairly quiet. She is missing hanging around Perranporth, stalking Andrew Whitehead and his fiancée. The fact that she can't drink tonight upsets her too, I think. We wander from one pub to another until we end up at the night club where Monopoly are performing. It's only 10 pm but it's completely overcrowded and very, very noisy. Tina's eyes light up – surprise, surprise! Who is leaning on the bar looking pretty? No other than Andrew Whitehead.

"What's he doing here?" I ask Tina.

She smiles happily. "Same as us, obviously. He's got good taste. He must be a Monopoly fan as well!" she exclaims. She suddenly looks so much livelier now. It is almost impossible to hold a conversation anyway so I just sit back and watch Tina with interest. When Ian offers to buy a round of drinks Tina volunteers to queue up at the bar. Nobody questions why! Taking my eyes off my friend I look around the large crowded room. How much cider have I had so far? I think, I am seeing things – over there, close to the stage is a group of people and guess who is among them? No way! It's Lance from next door! I am like glued to the spot. What is he doing here? Ian passes me my drink.

"Are you okay, Jen? You look a bit pale to me," he says, sounding really worried.

"I'm fine, Ian, honestly, couldn't be better," I assure him. Nothing matters anymore. I stare at Lance, my knight in shining armour. He seems to know a lot of people, both male and female. Then, without any warning, the massive room falls quiet as Monopoly are taking to the stage. Rapturous applause fills the venue when the first chord is struck.

"Good evening, ladies and gentlemen..." the lead singer begins, announcing the band's first song through the microphone. This must be Petroc Hayman. Lots of girls in the room start screaming as Petroc introduces the all-male band members. My eyes watch the well-dressed Lance. He's smiling, standing very close to a girl with long dark shiny hair. She is pretty, very slim and well-tanned. Monopoly are so loud that the beat goes right through my body. A man in jeans and a rugby shirt passes Lance a beer. He's older than the others but seems to be part of the group. I can feel Tina's elbow in my ribs.

"Hey, are you enjoying yourself?" she shouts at me.

"Yes, very much," I say enthusiastically. Petroc Hayman is singing, well, shouting, screaming, whatever you want to call it. The girl with the long hair appears to love it. She's jumping up and down, waving her hands, mouthing the lyrics as Petroc sings. Lance is not touching her. He is just watching, sipping his pint.

Tina's arm is around my waist now.

"What is it, Jen? Do you fancy Petroc Hayman or what?" she wants to know.

Instinctively I shake my head. How could I possibly fancy him?

"One of the other two then? I've noticed that you can't take your eyes off them," Tina continues.

I have a hard job to hear her.

"No, I don't fancy any of them," I confirm clearly.

"Andrew's gone," Tina informs me, as if I am interested. Lance is still here and that's all that matters to me at the moment. As the band finally takes a break Lance disappears from the crowd. I am hoping he will return so I am offering to buy Ian and Annette more drinks. They decline but Tina wants a Diet Coke. Fighting my way through the noisy crowd I am wondering how I can get closer to Lance. Then I spot him only metres away from the bar. He's talking to Monopoly's lead singer. I watch him offering to buy him a drink. His body language tells me that they must be good friends. It's very obvious that he knows him well. There is no doubt in my mind that it was Petroc Hayman who came to visit Lance on the day I saw him for the first time. In the bright, colourful disco light I study the two men's faces. They are like chalk and cheese – Lance with his immaculate dark complexion and handsome features and Petroc, naturally pale-skinned, blond, his thin hair held in place by wax and gel. While the well-built Lance appears very fit and strong, Petroc, despite being equally as tall, looks half his strength and size. He is perspiring after his most energetic performance on stage, his cheeks glowing. Just as I am finally being served the long-haired beauty joins the men at the bar. She is in the company of the other two band members but soon I watch her kissing Petroc.

"You alright? My coke is getting warm," Tina reminds me.

She seems seriously worried about me.

"Come on, Jen. What is it? I've never known you like this. You are completely, well, I don't know, mesmerised by something or someone," Tina tries to explain. Reluctantly I nod.

"Right. So who is it?" Tina asks.

Monopoly are back on stage and I can't see Lance anymore.

"It's Petroc Hayman," I lie easily.

"Thought so!" Tina announces victoriously.

"I didn't think he was your type but apparently he comes to our beach quite often so you may well get a chance to see him again," Tina tells me.

Like lightning I turn around.

"Our beach? Where does he live? What do you know about him?" I ask against the terribly loud music.

Tina smiles. She's got me now.

"Steady on, Jen. I don't know anything about him but people say he's around," Tina shouts back. The long-haired girl has returned to her position near the stage but I have lost sight of Lance.

Just after midnight the gig is over. Ian and Annette decide that they are ready to leave Newquay. Thankfully Tina is immediately prepared to drive back. I've had enough, too. On the way home to Hayle I hardly speak.

"She's dreaming of Petroc Hayman," Tina announces, pressing the gas pedal a little harder. Annette is too tired to react but Ian laughs.

"Petroc Hayman? Tough luck, Jen. He's engaged. I know his brother. He's big into surfing," he says to me.

I turn around in my seat.

"Do you know the Haymans well?" I want to know.

"No, but they do come down to the beach quite a bit," Ian confirms.

It's only when I get back to my grandparents' house that I pull the small note with the car registration number out of my shorts.

"I wonder if Petroc Hayman drives a red Fiesta…" I say to the piece of paper in front of me. I am tired and I have a headache from all the noise and the cider.

Sunday turns out to be another glorious day. I am not feeling too special at all but I am on duty at 7:30 am – "no rest for the wicked" as they say. With painkillers on board I cycle down to the car park to open up. Beyond the dunes the sea looks blue, very calm, almost Mediterranean. This time of morning the sky appears golden-pink, an absolutely incredible colour. Is it surprising that so many artists choose to live and work in Cornwall? It is just a magical place. I have often wondered what it must be like to live here all year round. Immediately I am reminded of Lance. No doubt he is at home, lying in, the lazy boy. None of my Cornish friends have to work this early on a Sunday morning.

By lunch time the car park is full. Tina has only just got up but she is not going to drive to Perranporth today. She's on her bike.

"Hi, Jen. How are you doing?" she asks me jovially.

"I'm alright, thanks," I reply a little lethargically.

"Is Don going to take over here this afternoon?" Tina wants to know.

"No, I don't think so. There's no point. We are full. I can cope on my own today," I explain quickly.

"Tristan, Jack and all are coming down later. I was just wondering if you could join us," Tina says then.

"Doubt it," I respond sharply.

Tina chains her bike to the fence.

"Petroc does not come here when it's busy," she suddenly says.

"How do you know?" I ask, much too eagerly for my liking.

"It's no secret, Jen. The guy is always around but he keeps well away from people. I just never thought

44

that you were interested, that's all," Tina answers truthfully.

"He must have friends in the area," I say.

"Yeah, suppose so. What do you see in him? I mean Andrew, yes. He's cool, you have to admit, but Petroc is not great. I don't think he's even got a good voice," Tina says shrugging. Then she pads me on the shoulder.

"You heard what Ian said – you are too late," she says. With that she's off to the beach.

I return to my shady hut. If Petroc does not come down here when it's busy, then I must come when it's quiet. He's friends with Lance and I am determined to meet him. The afternoon drags on but finally I am allowed to pack up. Although Tina and Co are expecting me to join them on the beach this evening I am on my bike home now. Gran and Grandad are out in the garden having a cup of tea.

It takes me less than a minute to find out why Grandad is grumpy. He is pointing to Max and Louisa's garden.

"Next door are having a barbeque. Not only do we get all the smoke over here but their son has been playing some awful music with the windows wide open. I've already been to see them once but I may have to go again," he mumbles.

Gran just sits there and says nothing. I am about to comment when a soft voice calls from the gate.

"I've got your plate here," we hear Louisa say. Gran and I turn around.

"Oh, thank you," Gran says getting up and taking her plate out of Louisa's slim fingers.

"The cake was delicious. Thank you so much. I had to hide it from our son though. He would have eaten the lot if I'd let him," Louisa tells us.

I would have loved to say, "Perhaps you would be kind enough to introduce him to me," but, of course, I do nothing.

Gran smiles proudly. "I am very happy to supply another cake – maybe for your son's birthday," she says cleverly.

"That would be great, thank you," Louisa replies politely before turning away.

Only seconds later Max appears at the gate.

"Hey, Richard," he calls over to Grandad, "I know you don't like the smell but how about a beer and a succulent sausage?" Max invites him.

Grandad feels visibly irritated and a bit embarrassed.

"No, thanks. We are going to have a proper dinner later on," he declines.

I could kill him. Why does he have to say no?

I look at Max who seems really put out now. How can anyone resist him? He is such an attractive man. My smile must have given my thoughts away as Max hands me the ice cold bottle of beer.

"You can have a glass of wine if you prefer," he offers softly.

Hesitantly I take the bottle from him.

"No, that's fine. Thank you," I say a little awkwardly.

"How about your grandmother?" Max enquires.

Gran has gone inside to prepare the meal.

"I'll go and ask her," I promise.

"Max, darling. I think, the meat needs turning," I hear Louisa shout. It appears that Lance is not around tonight. Carefully I approach Gran in the kitchen.

"Max is offering you a drink…" I start.

"Tell him, no, thank you. Richard does not want to become too friendly with the neighbours," she says straight away.

When I get back outside Max has returned to his barbeque.

"Nothing for Gran, thanks!" I call over into next door's garden. Max nods in the distance. I think he has got the message that my grandparents don't like him.

I sit down on the lawn and drink my beer. Why does Grandad have to be so hostile? Max and Louisa are really lovely people. For a moment it is very quiet but then I hear a car arriving next door. It's Monopoly blasting out of the open windows. My heart is beating faster. I am tempted to jump up to see who has come up the drive but I remain seated. The noise ceases instantly and I hear doors being slammed shut. Turning my head slightly I can see three people walking around the house towards the back garden – Lance, Petroc and the dark-haired beauty who had kissed him at the concert.

Gulping up the last drop of my beer I get up. It's now or never. Walking slowly to the gate I call over to Max.

"Thanks for the beer." None of the three youngsters even turn their heads.

Sitting at the table with my grandparents is real torture. I want nothing more than go up into my room and watch next door's party out of my window. Instead all I hear is Grandad rumbling on.

"I wonder how many more garden parties they are going to have this summer," he says angrily.

Gran smiles mildly.

"Well, they have to make the most of this weather. They will soon have to get used to the fact that this is not South Africa. Days like today are few and far between," she tells him.

"I wish that Max would mind his own business. I don't want him leaning over the gate all of the time inviting me for food and drinks," Grandad goes on.

"He's only being friendly," I pop up.

"I know that kind of friendly, dear. The next thing is that he wants to put up a wall, a conservatory, extension or whatnot and then he'll say he's always been kind to us so would we please agree to his plans. I know exactly how these people tick!" Grandad argues.

We watch thick blue smoke passing through my grandparents' garden.

"If you can't beat them, join them, I say," I comment absent-mindedly.

"Nonsense, dear. I am not going to join anyone!" Grandad insists.

It is nearly dark when I finally go upstairs. The neighbouring garden looks amazing. Louisa has decorated her lawn with candles and torches everywhere. I can just make out the faces of the guests. Petroc and his fiancée are sitting down on a blanket. Lance is standing up, glass in hand. Max has his arm around his wife. They are keeping warm near the barbeque. Everyone seems to have a good time. Watching them makes me feel a little jealous. There is something missing from this almost perfect picture – a girlfriend for Lance.

Later, in the bed, I think about Tina's words. If Petroc usually visits our beach when it's deserted then I should find it easy to approach him. If anyone knows that beach then it's me – and if Petroc is close friends with Lance then the only way is to meet him first. Sir Lancelot is by far too arrogant to speak to me!

When I get on my bike the next morning the car that arrived last evening is still in next door's drive. Guess what – it's an old red Fiesta with a very familiar registration plate! Well, Brownie points for Mr Monopoly – he has paid his parking fee as I requested.

Cycling along I am wondering if all the youngsters had a sleepover at Lance's house last night. *Seabreeze* is a large family home, ideal for that kind of thing. Deep in thoughts I arrive at the car park. I am a little early today but the first customers are already waiting in front of the barrier. It is promising to be another fantastic day for beaching. I take my money bag and let the cars in. Until about 11 am I hardly get any rest. We are not entirely full yet but I am retreating into my hut so that I can make a call to the café. One of the waiting staff will usually come out and look after the car park when I need a comfort break. I am about to press the buttons on my mobile phone when a shiny silver Mercedes arrives. Needless to say, I recognise the car immediately – it's Max and Louisa.

"Hi," I greet them smiling, very much hoping to find Lance in the backseat.

"Hi, you are the girl from next door, aren't you?" Max says, pushing his pricy sunglasses onto his head.

I ignore his slightly patronising remark and pass him a ticket. There is no one sitting in the back of the car, unfortunately. Max's good-looking face is frowning.

"Surely you are not going to charge me!" he exclaims.

What cheek? Only because he is my grandparents' neighbour! I feel a little nervous but I am determined to stand my ground.

"I'm ever so sorry but I have to. I only work here. It's not my car park," I explain truthfully.

"Come on, everyone knows it's your grandad's! We can call ourselves locals now," Max argues.

I have to say, I did not expect that.

The driver of the car behind the Merc is getting impatient.

"If you want have private conversation do later!" he suggests in broken English.

"It's £5 for locals too," I say as calmly as possible. Louisa passes her husband a £5 note.

"Come on, darling. The girl is only doing her job," she says sweetly.

Max shakes his head. Unwillingly he passes me the money but I can see that we have not heard the last of that yet. He drives on, totally oblivious to the foreign driver behind him who is making rude comments whilst waving a £10 note at me. I hand him his ticket and the change and make my call.

My mouth is so dry that I need a drink whilst I am at the café. Jake, Lauren and the new baby have just come in. While everyone is admiring Trevellyan I am wondering what to do. Should I ring Grandad and tell him what happened? Just in case I am not around when

Max complains to him? Or should I just ignore it and hope Max will forget about it? I order myself a Fanta before returning to my hut. The silver Mercedes is parked in the blazing sunshine. As more cars queue up to enter the car park it is time for me to take over again.

Don arrives at 2:30 pm for his shift. I have already sold the last available parking space, handing Don the sign reading *Car Park Full*.

"Well, the water looks inviting. Off you go, enjoy your swim," I hear Don say as I take my bag and wander off towards the busy beach.

Strangely enough I have not heard from Tina. The tide is far out so the beach looks even larger than it really is. Gazing across the wide blue bay I stroll along the upper part of the beach where the flat grey pebbles are. As the sun is beating down so strongly this afternoon many holidaymakers are seeking shelter among the large brownish-grey rocks which provide a little shade.

At the surf school Ian is teaching children at the water's edge. I don't know why watching him makes me wonder what Lance does on a day like today. Putting my sun hat on I scan the vast expanse of sand. Thankfully I cannot see Max and Louisa anywhere. Everyone seems so happy on the beach but I feel a little depressed. Having now reached the softer and less coarse sand I take my flip-flops off and stroll aimlessly along the beach. It is an exceptionally lovely day.

For a few minutes I just walk on, through the warm sand, my beach bag over my shoulder. There are several cafés along the shore, overlooking the beach and the today wonderfully calm sea. Every one of them is absolutely packed. On a day like this there is nowhere better in the world. This is the Cornish coast at its best, simply stunning, so very beautiful. Benign and rhythmic the waves are rolling in. This afternoon the water appears bright turquoise against the perfectly blue sky, the wide strip of golden sand and large grey rocks. Several lifeguards are out on their quad-bikes having a busy time warning people of the dangers of the incoming tide near the Hayle estuary.

Watching young children play in a clear pool that has formed around the emerging rocks I stop to take my mobile phone out. I must apologise to Tina. Not turning up last evening was not nice, I must admit. Impatiently I wait for her to answer her phone. It is not going to happen. She's either at Perranporth in the water or she does not want to hear from me. A little annoyed with myself about my ignorant behaviour last night I put my mobile away and wander on.

Looking back across the vast beach it is surprising how far I have walked without noticing it. Godrevy Lighthouse seems so small in the far distance. I am almost at the end of the three miles of famous golden sands, very close to the mouth of the estuary. This is where the dunes are really high. The sand here is particularly fine and soft, a whitish yellow in colour, a glittery sparkling powder... hang on, the couple up there, I seem to recognise them.

Halfway up the steep dunes I can clearly see two people sitting down, watching the sea. Both are wearing sunglasses and hats but I have no doubt that they are Petroc Hayman and his slim, sun-tanned fiancée. Marching on but not taking my eyes off them, I am wondering what's going on. The girl with the long dark hair is getting up. Her body language is telling me that she is not happy, in fact she looks furious. Petroc, still seated on the ground, his feet dug deeply into the sand does not move but I can definitely make out that he is arguing. Trying not to stop and stare I approach the water. Slowly I walk in until I am up to my knees in the clear, cold and salty sea, while watching with interest. The girl storms off. She has a hard job to climb up the dunes in the hot heavy sand. Petroc lets her go but then suddenly he follows on, right up to the top where I presume his car must be parked. His fiancée has got out of my view. I can just see him now. He's wearing very cool, colourful shorts and a plain white T-shirt. Eventually he disappears into the car park, too. So much for not coming to the beach when it's busy! And what about Lance? Why didn't he come? Maybe he doesn't like the beach?

At the mouth of the estuary the tide is coming in extremely fast. If I am not leaving this place very soon I will have to walk back across the top of the cliffs which will take me ages. Half running, half walking, I make my return journey along the crowded, rapidly shrinking beach.

Back at my grandparents' house I am glad that a few clouds have magically appeared on the horizon and neither Gran nor Grandad is spending any time in the garden. Perhaps I should not mention the incident at our car park earlier. I feel sure that Max won't come over and ring the doorbell to complain to Grandad about the charges.

After dinner Gran announces that she and Grandad are going down to the pub. It's one of their friend's surprise birthday party but Gran says it will be OK if I come as well. "No, thanks," I decline immediately. I simply don't fancy sitting around with the old dears tonight. Gran and Grandad leave around 8 pm and I am wondering what to do. No word from Tina or anyone else. I sit by the window texting Lolly in London. How quickly the weather can change in

Cornwall! It's really quite dark tonight. A wall of thick cloud has moved in and the wind has got up considerably.

Don't ask me why but around 9:30 pm I decide to take my bike for a ride down to the beach. Both the car park and the beach café are closed now. Apart from a few evening walkers the area looks fairly deserted. I am glad that I've got my sweater on. A strong south-westerly wind is blowing across the bay and it feels surprisingly cold. Hard to believe that it was so hot earlier in the day! With no sign of the security guard yet I lock my bike up near my little hut. Then I start walking through the dunes. I love the salty smell of the sea, the clean air and the wind ruffling up my hair. Tonight the tide is right in with the waves seeming unusually high. Soon there's hardly anyone left on the beach as it is getting darker. Above me the sky is suddenly looking ghostly, somehow threatening. Knowing how dangerous this beach can be at night I keep close to the high cliffs. The towering, rugged rocks appear black in the fading light.

When I was a child I was always afraid to go past the unstable-looking cliffs in the dark. My grandad claims to know every cave in the rocks and there are many! Holidaymakers love exploring these unusual dark chambers but only the locals know the really deep ones, the hidden, secret rooms in this massive granite coastline. Grandad used to tell me stories about them, very scary ones, too! So what am I doing here right now? The noise of the waves crashing onto the beach is deafening. Shells and stones are being tossed onto the shore. It's almost dark. Everyone has left. It certainly seems like there's no one around. What if I trip, break my ankle – it's silly being out here this late in the evening – and still I am walking on, my eyes directed heavenwards. Was that lightning over there in the distance? I stop, then walk on. Why? I can hear the rumble of thunder, quite faint at the moment but a storm is definitely on its way. I must return to my bike, ride home as fast as can but I am not turning back. Strangely undeterred I continue walking along the dark beach.

Suddenly, from out of nowhere, a person appears in front of me - no, that's not correct – a black figure emerges from the high rocks. I am startled. Instantly I can feel my heart beating faster and I stop walking, stunned. The light is so dim now that I can only guess it's a man. He's only a couple of steps away from where I am standing, in fact he is so close that he can't pass me without saying anything. Although I am panicking, frightened to death, I try hard to establish what he looks like. He's all dressed in black, wearing tracksuit bottoms and a hoody with the hood up, black skate-shoes. If this wasn't real I would think he's a ghost. He's slim, for a man not particularly tall.

"Hi," I utter – just for something to say, I suppose. He's no more than a stone's throw away from me now, and he makes no attempt to escape. As lightning strikes again I recognise his face, his distinctive features. I'm staggered. This must surely be a case of mistaken identity. I've seen this face before, on Saturday night and in the distance this afternoon. With the approaching storm continuing the sound of the mighty thunder seems closer. I take a deep breath.

"Collect £200 salary as you pass," I say bravely.

Petroc smiles for a mere second but then he looks distinctly annoyed. If he was hoping to stay incognito he has just realised that I've recognised him.

"What are you doing here?" he asks sternly.

His question surprises me to say the least.

"This is a public beach, isn't it?" I answer him with another question.

"Yeah, but at this time of night…" he starts.

"You don't own this place – no houses, no hotels. You can't charge!" I say daringly.

Petroc no longer finds me funny.

"It's a very dangerous beach, at night anyway. I'll walk you back to the car park," he offers, pointing in the opposite direction of where I am heading.

How incredibly patronising! He must think I'm a stupid schoolgirl or something.

"Come off your high horse, Petroc Hayman. I know this place better than most," I defend myself firmly. The black skate shoes are drawing nervous circles in the sand.

"I would appreciate it if you stayed away from here though," Petroc says aggressively, pointing towards the gap between the large rocks from which he had appeared so suddenly. Looks like he's not very good at handling his newly found fame. If he treats his fans like this he will soon have to go without them. His hostile attitude really rubs me up the wrong way. I'm starting to relax a little, enjoying this odd conversation.

"Your secret is safe with me. I won't tell anyone about the cave – if that's what you are afraid of," I tell him. The muscles in his young face are visibly tightening up.

It has started to rain, the wind blowing even stronger than before. I resolve not to walk any further but turn around and follow Petroc.

"What do you know about the cave?" he asks, slowly walking on.

I stay next to him, carefully considering my next answer.

"Everything," I simply lie, trying to increase my pace. My reply makes Petroc stop in his tracks.

"How often have you been here and when?" he asks urgently, fighting against the strong breeze.

"Not very often," I say vaguely. I realise that I am playing a dangerous game but if I want to meet Lance I'll have to carry on.

"And you haven't told anyone about it?" he asks quickly.

"No, I swear," I say and that is the truth because I don't really know what he is talking about. Although it is pitch dark by now – I can see that he is assessing me.

"What's your name?" he asks. It does not sound very friendly at all, the way he says it.

"Sue," I tell him. Susan is my middle name so I think I can get away with that.

"Listen… Sue," he says, taking a deliberate break between the two words. The rain is lashing down now and we are getting closer to my car park.

"I don't know if I can trust you. Tell me what you want, within reason, of course, to keep our secret," he says to me. What an offer! All I need to say is – I want to meet your friend Lance but obviously I can't do that.

"I don't want anything, nothing at all. I am not one of your crazy fans," I start but he interrupts me. "Tickets, money, CDs – I can arrange that for you but…" he says.

"You heard what I said. I am not interested in you, Monopoly or anything else. You have my word – I won't tell anyone about your cave. Okay?" I say and I like it that I am sounding so stroppy, quite confident now.

"And why would you do that?" he asks as we finally enter the car park.

"Because I am that kind of person, trust me," I reply firmly.

"Where do you live? It's freezing out here. Let me drive you home," Petroc offers pulling a set of keys out of his by now thoroughly wet tracksuit bottoms.

I am surprised that the security guard is not around and there is definitely no old Fiesta left in the car park either.

"Thanks, but I've got my bike here," I decline politely.

"It's too dark, wet and windy for cycling. I would be very pleased to drive you home. Look, we share a secret now. You can trust me, too," Petroc says kindly.

His voice sounds much softer all of a sudden.

"I'll take the bike. I don't want to be seen with you," I argue confidently. It really is cold in the car park tonight. I am shivering, and it's not just because of the temperature.

Petroc shakes his head. "Perhaps you are right," he concedes eventually.

I am about to run off to my bike when he grabs my sweater.

"I'd like to see you again, Sue – at the cave, tomorrow night," he says.

This invitation makes me shudder even more.

"I don't know…" I say hesitantly.

I have to admit, I don't like the idea.

"Come on. If you expect me to trust you, you must trust me. I'll meet you at 10 pm – no matter what weather. Can you make that?" he asks.

"I'll try," I say.

Then he offers me his hand. A little reluctant at first I accept it.

"I'll see you tomorrow!" I confirm.

I don't think I've ever ridden home this fast. Totally out of breath, wet through and shaking from head to toe I arrive at my grandparents' house, my heart still beating like a drum in my chest. Was this all a bad dream or reality? Gran and Grandad have long gone to bed so I creep upstairs, hoping they won't hear me.

Needless to say I can't sleep at all tonight. I have made a promise that I cannot break. Under no circumstances must I tell anyone about Petroc's cave but what if he is dangerous? Never in my life have I met anyone in secret. This man is a complete stranger. If he rapes or even kills me, then nobody will know about it. Grandad says that these caves can be many metres deep. Is it really worth risking my life for someone I've only seen from a distance? Surely there must be an easier way of meeting Lance. I've got myself into such a mess, I can hardly believe it.

As morning arrives I get up. I feel absolutely shattered. Gran and Grandad are already downstairs in the kitchen. Their voices and the smell of fried bacon fill the entire house. Yawning I join them.

"Good morning. Did you have a good party last night?" I ask as I take my seat at the table.

"We did until Max turned up," Gran starts to explain. Grandad is pacing up and down the kitchen now.

"What happened?" I enquire, trying to assess the weather conditions through the steamed-up kitchen window.

"We were minding our own business," Grandad begins, his face looking as dark and fierce as that thundery sky last night.

"I went up to the bar to order a round of drinks when Next Door approached me from behind. He offered to buy me a drink, then takes me to one side," Grandad says.

I can guess what's coming but I don't say anything.

"He told me that you charged him £5 for the car park and that he didn't think that that was fair considering we were neighbours and so on..." Grandad continues.

He is furious, I can tell.

"Anyway, I gave him a piece of my mind. Who does he think he is expecting special treatment? I told him to stop inviting us, offering food and drink across the fence. I've declared war on the bloke – I knew he was going to be bad news from the start," Grandad says, finally sitting down.

My head bowed I listen.

"You did the right thing, Jen," Gran tells me, stroking my back.

"Oh, yes, definitely!" Grandad confirms immediately.

I am not so sure and I am not hungry. Although I feel a little sick I try to eat my breakfast. What have I done? As soon as I can I leave the table to check the weather outside. It's not great, very overcast, cool and still quite windy.

"No need to go down to the car park too early today," Grandad comments.

The urge to get out of the house makes me pick up my jacket.

"It's okay. I'm ready now and I shall open up as normal," I insist.

Grandad shrugs his shoulders but he does not stop me.

Nervously I cycle down to the beach. Gazing down the highly acclaimed three miles of golden sands I am wondering if I will still find the spot where I bumped into Petroc last night. My knowledge of the cliffs and their caves isn't that good really. From the distance the large granite rocks look all the same. Slowly I open up the barrier. I was so cold last evening that I failed to find out what type of car Petroc was driving. What's happened to the old red Fiesta? Perhaps that is not even his car. It could be his fiancée's or even Lance's? Surely Sir Lancelot won't be seen dead in a vehicle like that? I notice that I am shaking. I cannot trust Petroc but I am not prepared to let him down either.

By 9 am a couple of cars arrive but it is generally very quiet today. The hours just won't pass. At lunch time it starts raining again. I get my mobile phone out of my bag and ring Don.

"Don't bother coming out," I tell him. He seems to be happy with that. Gran's sandwiches, so lovingly prepared for me each morning, remain untouched. I can't eat, not today. I feel so terribly nervous. My mobile announces a text. It's from Tina who is wondering if I would go out with her tonight. With trembling fingers I decline, explaining that I've got something else on, which is true. I will have to tell my grandparents that I am going out with Tina though and hopefully they won't ask any further questions.

The afternoon drags on. By 2 pm I close the car park as it continues raining steadily. I return home, helping Gran with the housework. We are preparing the dinner together, talking about this and that but avoiding the subject of "next door". Grandad has calmed down, too. I must force myself to eat tonight. Outside the weather remains poor.

"I'll give you a lift wherever you need to go this evening," Grandad offers when I tell him that I am planning to go out.

"No, thanks, Grandad. Tina will take care of me. I don't have far to go on the bike and if it continues raining she can always drop me home. I expect it is going be late tonight," I say nervously.

"As you wish," Grandad eventually concedes but he does not look very happy.

Yes, I do wish. I leave the house much earlier than I intended, butterflies in my stomach. It's dry at the moment but still cloudy and very windy. Just like yesterday I cycle down to the beach, lock my bike to the fence near the hut and start walking towards the dunes. I'm well aware of the fact that I am by far too early but I need time to find that gap in the rocks and I am terribly nervous. I am wearing a washed-out baseball cap, jeans, old trainers and a thick sweater. Not surprisingly there is nobody on the beach, not in this weather. The sand under foot is sticky, wet and heavy, my footprints leaving deep ditches as I stroll along. I must be careful, don't want to be seen. Like a criminal I check all around me. It is eerily quiet apart from the waves crashing onto the beach, leaving a thick white residue on the dark sand as they recede. I can just make out that there's someone walking a dog in the distance. Approaching the black rocks I try and hide between the high granite walls as I look for the opening, smudging my footprints as I go along. The rain has started yet again. If only I knew where Petroc's particular rock actually is! Checking my watch I am wondering if he is already in the cave. Would he be looking out for me? Unsure if I should not simply give up and turn back I pull my old baseball cap deeper into my face, shivering. I am so close to the high dark rocks now that I can touch them. They feel cold, wet and slippery. A musty smell of moss, salt and dampness travelling up my nose I continue searching. Under the grey sky it's getting darker very fast. I really don't know exactly where it is, that special cave.

"Psst!" I hear a human voice behind me.

My heart filled with fear and anxiety I turn around. It's Petroc, dressed in black again, leaning on one of the slimy, smelly rocks. It annoys me thinking he must guess that I don't know my way around.

He reaches out, offering me his cold slim hand. Then he quickly pulls me behind a large rock, not saying a word.

"Hi," I whisper nervously.

Not being able to see his face properly frightens me. We enter a small gap between a couple of awesome-looking rocks. It is completely dark inside and I am so scared, I can hardly proceed without breathing heavily. Creeping on all fours we pass through a dark tunnel. The strong odour of the sand and ancient rock is overpowering in the narrow passageway. What am I doing here? Petroc is leading the way. At the very end of the tunnel I can see some light, candle light! All of a sudden the inside of the black rock opens up. We can almost stand upright now. With the help of the candle light we wind ourselves around a sharp corner. I am gobsmacked. This is absolutely amazing. The salty, muddy smell seems to be magically disappearing as we creep along. I can feel a strange kind of warmth, the air thick with the fragrance of incense. Before me lies a hall, as large as my bedroom at home. The dome-like space is filled with candles everywhere and there's a crucifix attached to the back wall. This is no longer a cave, it's a church! In front of the crucifix stands a keyboard, a modern, expensive-looking one. Wooden boxes propped up by bricks are placed all around the surprisingly dry cave. The sand under our feet is hard, very clean. This secret hall is fascinating as well as spooky. My whole body feels numb with fear and wonder. Admiring the incredible effect of the bright candlelight in this most beautiful and unusual cave I turn around. Petroc is smiling.

"You've never been here before, have you? You lied to me last night," he says calmly.

My eyes directed to the crucifix I nod. I feel awful now, don't know what to say to him. He steps forward to the keyboard.

"This is where I get my inspiration, this is my spiritual home, my office," he announces proudly.

Then he strikes up a chord. The acoustics are unbelievable, so strong, so church-like.

"I've written lyrics and composed music here," he continues, looking up from his keyboard.

I am still standing in the middle of the holy cave, unable to move. Petroc is playing away but not singing.

"Take a seat," he invites me, pointing to one of the wooden boxes.

I do as I am told, shaking like a leaf, watching Petroc intently. He has finally taken his black hood off. His blond hair looks wet, sticking to his head. In the flickering candle light his eyes are strikingly blue. He's definitely not my type but at this very moment there is something about him that attracts me. The way his slim fingers touch the keys almost tenderly, the most peculiar smile on his pale face – I take another deep breath.

"When did you find this place?" I ask.

It is surprising how much heat the candles create. I am feeling quite hot in my thick woolly jumper.

Petroc leaves the keyboard in order to join me on the creaking old box. He's sitting close to me now.

"A long time ago," he replies carefully.

Instinctively I jump up. I am afraid of him. The aura of this cave has got me in its spell and I don't like it. Something or someone makes Petroc's sparkling blue eyes go right through me. I feel uncomfortable as well as excited. It seems that Petroc is aware of my mixed emotions but he does not speak. The expression on his young but very manly face remains serious.

"I have not told anyone about this, not even Jamie and Pete, my band mates. I do a lot of work from home as well. When I come here nobody knows where I really am. I always used to tell my fiancée that we were practicing. She has never questioned me," he explains after a while.

I frown doubtfully. From my reaction it becomes clear that I don't believe him.

"You must share this secret with somebody other than me!" I tell him.

His slim fingers are reaching out for me now.

"Yes, I do – with God," he says softly. Once again my eyes are directed towards the crucifix.

"With God?" I ask, shaking my head.

The expression on Petroc's face shows that he has recognised the mockery in my words. Tiny pearls of sweat are building up on his forehead. Clearly something is affecting or upsetting him but I am too scared to ask any further questions. I refuse to take his hand but I sit down again, next to him. His odd personality is strangely intriguing.

Then he gets up, walks past his keyboard and opens one of the heavy wooden boxes. Out come a bottle of red wine and two plastic glasses. It's a bottle with a screw top so it only takes Petroc seconds to open it.

"Why have you asked me to come here?" I want to know.

My entire body is trembling with fear. What does this man want from me?

Smiling Petroc passes me one of the glasses.

"When I bumped into you last night, God spoke to me," he declares solemnly.

If I was frightened before then I am now beside myself with panic. This rock musician could be mad, completely deranged, dangerous. How can I get out of here? I can hardly hold my glass still.

"Why are you so afraid? You can trust me," Petroc says, raising his glass.

I have no answer to that.

"Cheers. The fact that you have agreed to come here tonight shows me that you must have felt it too," Petroc continues calmly.

"Felt what?" I ask carefully.

"God sent you on that walk last evening because he wanted you to meet me," Petroc explains.

I take a large sip of red wine, almost choking.

"That's nonsense, Petroc," I argue.

"Then tell me why you were on the beach last night – remember, this is a place of trust," he says.

"I wanted to be on my own for a while, take time out to think. There was nothing religious, mystical or magical about it," I say in as cold a voice as possible.

Suddenly I feel Petroc's arm around my shoulders.

"Exactly, you may not have realised it but God sent you on that way – to meet me," he insists.

"I want to go now, please, Petroc. This is enough," I tell him angrily. With that I am on my feet, ready to leave this fascinating but scary cave. Deep down I am still afraid of him.

"You are not telling the truth, Sue. You've come here tonight for a reason," Petroc says firmly.

"You are engaged to be married, Petroc. If you are a devout Christian why do you lure another woman into this cave, tell me all this stuff and go on with your spiritual rubbish. Get a life and come to your senses!" I blast out at him, surprising myself with my deliberate outburst.

"God has prevented me from making the wrong choice, Sue. Yesterday afternoon he made me break the engagement to Liz and in the evening he sent you!" Petroc clarifies the situation.

I would have loved to tell him that I saw him quarrelling with his fiancée in the dunes but I decide not to.

"Why have you split up? And I want the truth!" I demand eagerly.

The strain on the musician's young face tells me that the answer hurts.

"I believe Liz has been cheating on me – with my best friend," he eventually continues.

Lance? It is on the top of my tongue but at the very last minute I restrain from commenting.

"You believe or you are sure?" I ask him.

He refills my glass, indicating for me to sit down next to him again.

"We, Liz and I, were invited to a barbeque at my friend's parents' house. We had a great evening and we were going to stay the night. Liz and I were in one room. She must have thought I was sleeping but I watched her creep out in the middle of the night..."

Bowing his head he adds, "She did not return for ages... Can you imagine how I felt? I was lying there wondering what to do. Then God spoke to me," Petroc says, his voice weakening.

He empties his plastic glass in one go.

"What did he say?" I ask. For the first time since I've been here I am starting to feel slightly more relaxed.

"He said, 'Let her go'. She does not really love you. You have deserved better," Petroc replies.

I smile mildly.

"So what about your friend? Does God think it is right for him to take your fiancée away from you?" I enquire, mocking him again.

Petroc remains serious.

"God will deal with my friend. I can rely on that. God deals with all who betray my trust," he says sharply.

It's only now that I notice that he is playing with my hair, ever so gently.

"I am sorry, Petroc, but I think you are crazy," I say to him. The wine has gone to my head but I am trying hard to stay in control.

"I want to play a song for you," he offers then. From under the keyboard he pulls out a handwritten list.

"You choose," I quickly say, not knowing what to expect. Petroc gets up, pulls another, much stronger box towards his keyboard and sits down. It is so hot in his church now that I have to take my sweater off. Petroc simply plays. The piece has a rather long, complicated instrumental introduction but then he begins to sing and it sounds fantastic. I am like spellbound, glued to the changing expressions on his face as he puts all his emotions into this song. He's good, really good. Why doesn't he go solo? His blue eyes look at me lovingly as he is singing and my cold heart begins to melt. I smile. I can't help myself. I feel like being in another world. It's all so unreal, so unbelievably warm. I don't want the song to end but it does.

"Did you write that here?" I ask Petroc. He nods proudly.

"It's incredible, very beautiful, moving, not like your Monopoly stuff at all," I remark.

I walk over to the keyboard. What is happening to me? Ever so slowly Petroc gets up, he steps forward until he is very close to me. We look into each other's eyes, creating a bond, an agreement that I never thought possible. My right hand touches his hoody. I am still afraid but my fear is crumbling. Willingly I close my eyes and I feel his kiss, very gentle, passionate but not demanding. He is holding me tight, so tight that I can hardly breathe. This is madness. There must have been something in the wine, a dangerous drug, I am sure of it.

"The candles are burning down. We've got to leave," Petroc whispers tenderly.

"Yes," I say.

He lets me go, opens the box that he has just used as a piano stool and passes me a torch. Meticulously he prepares his church for the off, extinguishing the candles, removing the powerful battery from his keyboard, locking all the boxes. I have no idea what the time is but I feel good, somehow happy. With him leading the way we return to the beach.

"Please let me drive you home tonight," he offers as we emerge from the awesome rocks. It is raining heavily and it is pitch dark.

"You've been drinking and I have my bike," I reply.

In silence we walk back to the car park, Petroc's slim arm around my shoulders.

"The church must remain our secret. Please promise me that, and I want to know more about you, where you live, what you do," Petroc says when we reach our destination.

I shake my wet head.

"No, whatever happened tonight will be our secret but I cannot do it again," I insist.

Then I run off to my bike.

"Sue!" I hear Petroc's voice calling behind me but I jump on and cycle home as fast as I can.

He is not following me for which I am eternally grateful.

Despite all the excitement I am sleeping well, so well in fact that Gran has to wake me up the next morning.

"Looks like you had a great night out," she comments kindly. I am quickly gathering my thoughts in case she asks me where I've been. Thankfully she doesn't – and she has arranged for Don to do the morning shift at the car park!

The weather is considerably better today but I am confused. I must put last night's experience behind me as hard as it may seem. Tina turns up at the car park unexpectedly and I manage to avoid the subject of Petroc Hayman.

"We are going over to the "*Sandsifter*" tonight. Do you fancy coming along, too?" Tina wants to know once she has returned from visiting Ian at the surf school.

I agree to go but I don't really feel like spending time with my old friends at the moment. It's something to do, I suppose, something to take my mind off Petroc – and Lance who I have not seen since that fateful night in his parents' house.

The takings of the day have not been bad so I can afford to go out to the *Sandsifter* bar tonight. I am getting ready early as Tina has invited us for starter drinks at her house before moving on to the famous bar and night club at the other end of our long beach.

"Make sure you take a sweater with you. It's a bit chilly out on the patio at night" has been Tina's advice this afternoon.

As I pick up my woolly jumper I am reminded of last night. The very slightly damp wool has taken on a surprisingly pleasant fragrance, a mixture of spicy incense and Petroc's aftershave. I am trying to tell myself that I don't like him but I am caressing the sweater lovingly as I take it out of my wardrobe.

At *Seabreeze* more building works have been going on all day long. Several vans are still parked outside and Louisa has been over to see Gran to apologise. Eventually I take both my handbag and my jumper in readiness to go out. Before I leave I simply cannot help looking out of my window, always hoping to catch a glimpse of Lance in the back garden. Is it true that he is cheating on his best friend? Why do I think that he is so perfect, just because he is good-looking? I say goodbye to my grandparents and cycle to Tina's house. As usual when Tina plans a night out there is a large crowd of people gathering around her small bedroom consuming alcoholic drinks. I take a seat on the floor, the only available space as it seems. Whilst everyone is talking my eyes spot part of a newspaper that is lying on a shelf underneath Tina's coffee table. The entertainment page has been folded over. To my great surprise it's Petroc Hayman's young face that is staring at me. There is a write-up about Monopoly's gig in Newquay last Saturday. I am desperately trying to read it but I do not want to be caught out.

An hour later we are moving on to the *Sandsifter*, the largest bar and dance venue on our beach. Tina tells me that there will be a new band playing tonight. Everyone appears to be really excited by the prospect of some fresh blood on the local music scene. Needless to say, the only reason why we are here is Andrew Whitehead. He and his band members who are considering themselves experts have come to see what the "Shellseekers" are all about. I can see that Tina is annoyed because Andrew has brought his future wife along this evening. Ian and Annette are mingling with the surfing crowd many of whom tend to regularly frequent the *Sandsifter* rather than the smaller bars at the other end of the beach. We are enjoying a round of drinks before the Shellseekers take to the large stage that has been prepared for them.

After a while I am a little bored with their style of music. Trying to escape the monotonous rhythm I am wandering out onto the patio. I feel the need to get some fresh air, get away from my friends. The evening sun is making one last appearance, throwing rays of bright orange across the beautiful sandy beach and the deeply blue bay. Standing on top of the high cliffs watching fishing boats returning to the estuary makes me realise how much I like Cornwall. I can't help thinking of last night, of Petroc and his strong beliefs. It is getting chilly, just as Tina anticipated, and I slip my sweater on. A glass of cider in my hand I try to recall last night's events when I hear the sound of a familiar voice. There is a group of men talking in the background. I hold my breath. *Don't turn around* I tell myself. Forcing my eyes to keep observing the activities out at sea I try and listen to the conversation behind me.

"I've written a new piece which I think will be ideal for next weekend," I hear Petroc say, only yards away from me.

"Can we have a listen then?" another man asks.

"Yeah, sure. If the Shellseekers will let me borrow their keyboard I'll play it right now," Petroc offers. It appears that his suggestion is not being taken seriously, it just causes loud laughter among the others. I dare not turn around.

"Jen? Jen, are you out here?" Tina's sharp voice disturbs my thoughts. Unfortunately she has spotted me. Instinctively I turn, now having to face the men behind me. There are three of them, all wearing sun glasses. It's Monopoly! Through his cool shades Petroc smiles at me but he does not say anything.

"Come on in. It's absolutely freezing out here. You've missed the best songs," Tina says while pushing me back into the overcrowded beach club.

Ian has bought me another drink.

"Ladies and gentlemen," the female lead singer of the Shellseekers announces a couple of minutes later, "I hope you have enjoyed our very first gig this evening – but now it is my honour and privilege to introduce to you someone who has recently performed on much larger stages than this – Mr Petroc Hayman," she says smiling.

Judging by the amount of applause the crowd can't wait to receive him.

"Petroc is here as a guest tonight but he has asked if he could play just one song for you. It's Monopoly's brand-new single *Candle light*."

With that the huge room turns remarkably quiet. Petroc, still in sunglasses, slowly takes a seat at the keyboard. I cannot believe it. He is going to play the song he played for me last night.

Ignoring Tina who is watching Andrew Whitehead kissing his fiancée I push my way to the front of the crowd. Standing near the stage I feel millions of goose pimples coming up as Petroc starts singing. Jamie and Pete, Monopoly's other two band members, keeping their distance behind him, are soon producing ad hoc backing vocals. How could Tina say Petroc doesn't have a good voice? I watch his lips, the lips that have kissed mine so tenderly last night, his hands that have held me tight but then I spot him in the crowd – Sir

Lancelot. He looks gorgeous as usual. He's smartly dressed and it appears that he's listening to Petroc's lyrics with interest. All of a sudden the world around me starts spinning. Petroc's song seems so much shorter than last night but the crowd is screaming appreciatively. They are loving it. Seemingly from out of nowhere Liz jumps onto the stage and kisses Petroc wildly. Everyone is applauding, apart from me. I just stand there like a lemon, doing nothing. Petroc and his band members bow, enjoying the continuing applause.

"Wow – that was a bit different!" Tina says which means praise indeed.

"Yes," I respond slowly.

"Oh dear," says Tina, putting her arm around me.

"It has hit you badly, hasn't it? I have to admit he was fantastic tonight," she goes on.

With a sad expression on my face I follow her to the bar. Liz is there with Petroc. I can see Jamie and Pete with what appear to be their girlfriends but where is Lance? Pretending to go to the toilet I leave the noisy room once more. It's almost dark outside and I notice that the seagulls have stopped squawking. Only very few couples are still out on the patio. I wish I could just escape, go home but I can't let Tina down, not this evening. As I am about to return to the crowd my heart misses a beat. Am I dreaming or is that the attractive Lance in the corner there, texting away? Like rooted to the spot I stare at him. *Go on, talk to him, this is your chance, a brilliant opportunity, introduce yourself – hi, I am your new neighbours' granddaughter, I've seen you in the garden next door, nice to meet you...* My inner voice is telling me how to go about it but I do absolutely nothing – just like Tina was with Andrew – tongue-tied, too shy.

Although I must have stood quite close to him for several seconds he has not taken the blindest bit of notice. Not even looking up he drops his mobile phone back into the pocket of his classy leather jacket and returns to the bar.

"Damn," I whisper and follow him.

"Sue!" I hear someone calling behind me but as it is not normally my name I do not react. It is incredibly noisy in the bar area now. Desperately fighting my way through the crowds I am looking for Tina. The stage has been transformed into a dance floor whilst I have been outside. Underneath my feet the floorboards are bending to the heavy beat of the disco music. Several young people are rocking the night away but still I cannot see any of my friends. Then I spot the beautiful Liz in her vibrant red dress. She is pulling Petroc up onto the dance floor. As he continues wearing his aviator-style shades I cannot make out the expression on his face but he appears unwilling. At this very moment someone in the crowd is shooting a photograph of the couple. Petroc is furious, I can tell. I watch him pushing the dancers around him out of the way, trying to catch the photographer. Within seconds panic breaks out. Fortunately the DJ is stopping the music so that the crowd begins to disperse in all directions. Totally oblivious to what is happening around me I keep observing proceedings from the sidelines. Jamie and Pete have come to Petroc's aid but Lance is no longer around.

Suddenly I feel an arm around my shoulders. "Phew, your Petroc causes quite a stir around here..." Tina says laughing.

Although I am glad that she has found me I do not like her comment.

"Let's go home," I suggest quickly.

The next morning an early sunrise suggests that it will be a brilliant day again and with that the car park is filling up rapidly. Jake has come over from the café to supply me with ice cream. Everyone is so kind to me. A few rude drivers are a small price to pay for such a pleasant and easy holiday job. Playing nervously with my moneybag I am thinking of Petroc and I am starting to understand why he likes secrets so much. With Monopoly's increasing success come responsibilities. There will be criticism, unwanted publicity, paparazzi... personally, I would not want any part of that. I am prepared to keep our secret but nothing more. Getting to know Lance is not the be all and end all, particularly not if he is such a cheat anyway.

Licking my delicious Cornish ice cream I am sitting in my little hut minding my own business. I am completely unaware that a shiny silver Mercedes has arrived outside. Not paying much attention I get my moneybag ready as I approach the car. The driver of the vehicle is not its owner – it's Lance! In the passenger seat next to him is a woman but it is not Liz! The gorgeous Lance is waving a £5 note at me. My heart sinks. Is this a set-up by the scheming Max or just an innocent visit to the beach? Lance's attractive smile confuses me.

"Hi," he says casually, handing me the bank note.

I am considering my position. *Take it* a small voice inside my head tells me but I hesitate. If I charge the father I must charge the son...

"It has not gone up, has it?" Lance asks, still holding the flimsy fiver in his immaculate fingers.

"Keep it. You are my grandad's next door neighbour – I won't charge you but don't tell anyone," I say.

Now it's Lance who looks confused.

"Thanks," he says and with that he hands the money back to his passenger and drives forward.

Well, I've met him – not quite in the way I wanted to but at least he may recognise me in the garden next time. As no other cars are arriving I watch him and his female passenger taking their beach bags out of the boot. I am trying hard to hide my interest but I am dying to know who that lucky woman is who will be able to spend a day on the beach with Lance. She's not quite as perfect a match for the handsome Sir Lancelot as Liz but she is also of dark complexion, slim and very athletic-looking. Once Lance has locked the car they slowly walk towards the dunes. Neither of them is smiling but they seem to be talking.

It is time for me to deal with another customer.

"Five pounds, please!" I say almost automatically, sounding like a robot. As I return to the hut I receive a text from Lolly in London. She has heard from Paul. He has sent her a letter saying that he has fallen in love with a girl in Australia and that their relationship is over. Poor Lolly – and she has been working so hard to earn money for her trip down under. *Come to Cornwall* I text her back, regretting the invitation straight away. Life can be so complicated.

Don arrives for his stint at 3 pm. As the silver Merc is still in the car park I decide to spend an hour on the beach as well. It's not as busy as at the weekends but I cannot see Lance and his lady-friend anywhere. They may have gone for a walk, visited one of the many beach bars or gone for a swim. I stroll along, dreaming, imagining Lance kissing his girlfriend. In my mind's eye I can see them having fun and I feel terribly jealous.

Everyone is down by the water's edge as the tide is coming in but I am walking, barefoot, close to the cliffs, high up where the larger, rounder pebbles are and where the sand is quite deep. As I am surveying the rocks, I suddenly realise that I must be somewhere in the area of Petroc's church. With the sun beating down the sand is heating up considerably. I put my flip-flops on in order to protect my feet. Dropping my beach towel and personal belongings close to the enormous wall of rock I decide to look for the entrance to the cave. How can it be so difficult finding that gap in the rocks at daytime?

Perhaps I should not be here. I must not be seen. There are too many people around. My hands carefully examining the cool grey stone I hesitate once more. I must be close, very close – and then I can clearly make out the narrow gap. Checking all around me I quickly slip in between the massive wall of sparkling solid granite. Immediately I duck, entering the long tunnel. It is difficult for my eyes to adjust to the dark and it is scary, really scary. Without Petroc showing me the way it is so much worse but I do remember where he is hiding his emergency lighter.

Soon I reach the ledge in the rock where Petroc keeps it. My hands are desperately searching for the tiny plastic bag that contains the lighter but I cannot find it. Panicking I step forward into the pitch dark. This is no good, I must return, get out of here before I injure myself on the sharp edges of the rocks. I can hear myself breathe. The slightest sound seems so much louder, clearer, down here. What am I doing? Without the lighter or at least the torch on my mobile phone I must not proceed. It is very cold in the cave and so incredibly dark. My shoulders unprotected from the fast dripping rocks I continue. I am guided by nothing but the faint smell of incense as I creep forward. Go back, stop, I am telling myself but I move on. Unbelievably I have reached the corner where the passageway becomes larger. Having got used to the dark I touch the damp walls around me. Not far now. My back is aching. I am tense, having held my body in a stooped position for much too long. The sand under foot feels suddenly harder, drier. I must be close to my destination.

I am making a confident leap forward when my foot is hitting something. In severe pain I scream out loud. It's the echo of the great hall that tells me that I have arrived at the church. Whatever I have stepped on has caused some damage. Instinctively I bend down, my hands touching my injured foot but it is too dark to see any blood. The worrying fact is that I can smell it, a distinctively ferrous odour on my fingers.

The pain subsides slightly as I manage to make out the contours of the crucifix. Surely there must be matches somewhere? All I want is leave a message for Petroc but I cannot even write anything into the sand, it is simply too dark. I am shivering, very frightened. How long have I been in here now? It seems like ages. What if I don't find my way back? Is there enough oxygen down here? Breathing heavily I try not to panic. Touching the rugged sides of the rocks like a blind woman I detect the boxes, all locked, of course, but at least they offer me a place to sit down, catch my breath, come to my senses.

Matches, matches is all I can think of at the moment. There seemed to be plenty of them around when I was here with Petroc – and candles. He had spare candles scattered around the boxes, not locked away. This is spooky, unreal. I am not normally religious but full of fear I whisper, "Please, God. Let me find my way back and grant me some matches, matches."

Then, suddenly, I become aware of a noise, a very hollow, disconcerting sound. My heart is beating so loudly that it must surely echo straight out onto the beach. Did Grandad say that these caves can collapse sometimes, without warning? Just like that, in broad daylight? And there it is again, that awful sound. It's not creaking, not thunderous, not like something breaking. It definitely sounds like someone coughing. I jump up. This cannot be happening. There is a brief flickering of light – and now it is coming closer but I have nowhere to go. All I can hope is that it is Petroc. It must be Petroc. No one else knows about this chamber. The shadow on the wall tells me that someone is approaching. Then I hear voices, two voices, quite clearly, one male, one female. What is the time? Who could it be? I have no chance to think about it. The voices are too close now. I leave my position and hide in a recess, right underneath the crucifix, a very narrow ridge in the rocks. This is the only hiding place I can see well enough in the dim light of the approaching torch.

Never in my entire life have I been so frightened. Here I am, trapped underground in a dark prison, and if I am going to be attacked there will be no way out.

Nobody knows where I am. If anyone finds my beach bag they may assume I have drowned in the sea, been kidnapped... It does not bear thinking about.

I don't get any further time to worry. By now the church is well lit and two persons are entering. I recognise them instantly. In order not to scream out loud I make a fist and hold it in front of my dry mouth. The strong beam of the large, modern torch is being sent all around the walls. Holding my breath I squeeze myself deeper into the rocks.

"Oh, my God! It's a church!" the woman exclaims. She is holding on tightly to the male, surely 30 years her senior, at least. His short silvery-grey hair is shining in the torch light.

"How did you know about this? It's amazing," she continues, quite in awe. Her long dark hair looks damp.

"I've known for years that this cave exists but I didn't know that it is someone's place of worship now," Max says nervously.

"Someone could still be down here. We'd better leave, quickly," Liz suggests.

She is dressed in nothing but a skimpy bikini and she looks petrified. I can see that she is shaking, almost as much as I am.

"Look, Max. There's blood in the sand. It looks fresh," she discovers then.

Max is directing the light onto the spot where I hurt myself, just minutes before they arrived. "There can't be anyone else in here, no one would find the way without a torch, without the knowledge..." Max replies shaking his head.

"But somebody must own all this stuff, the boxes..." I detect that Liz's voice has changed, so frightened is she.

"Relax. You can trust me. I have promised you that I will find a place where we can meet in secret." Max says softly.

Liz looks unsure. Reluctantly she puts her arms around him. He's wearing shorts-type swimming trunks and a white polo shirt. "I wish we didn't have to do this," she whispers, stroking him.

I am so close that I can hear every word she is saying. Max drops the torch onto one of the boxes and kisses her, very long and passionately. Having to watch it almost makes me vomit. My stomach is turning at the thought of what else may be about to happen. Shocked but somehow fascinated my cold fingers are digging into the rock as Max pulls Liz to the ground.

"You are so beautiful, darling," he tells her. I am forced to watch his nimble fingers undo her bikini top. Heaven help me, I don't want to see this. For a split second I close my eyes. When I reopen them I can see clothing strewn all over the church. Totally consumed by sexual desire the two lovers are lying in the sand. I can hardly breathe. The wish to simply pop up from my hiding place becomes stronger in me but all I can do is listen to them from close distance. Max's aging body is still in good shape and he is naturally an experienced lover. What is happening in front of me seems like a scene from a steamy romance on television. I have never watched anyone having sex in real life and I don't want to either but I am forced to stay where I am. Hanging on to the cold rock I feel like fainting as the illegitimate affair comes to a climax. Liz is screaming with pleasure until Max forbids her to carry on.

"Stop. They may hear you on the beach!" he tells her.

"Oh, darling, that was wonderful," enthuses Liz as Max gets up.

"Let's light some candles," he suggests.

I watch the naked Max walk over to where he has deposited his torch and I duck deeper into the tiny space in the recess. My knees have ceased up, my injured foot is throbbing and I need the toilet but I can do nothing but hold on.

"Petroc suspects that something is up, you know," Liz says then.

I can tell that she is freezing. She is crawling along in the turned up sand in order to fetch her lover's polo shirt. Thankfully she is making some attempt to cover herself up.

"You will have to string him along for a while. I can't leave Louisa so soon after the move," Max replies returning to his young mistress and sitting down next to her.

"But, Max, we can't go on like this either. This cave is fantastic, exciting, amazing – but we can't come here all the time if we want to be together," Liz responds.

Max's strong, mature hands are stroking her slim legs.

"I know, darling. I am going to buy something, a small house or an apartment, somewhere for us to move to when we are free. It takes time..." he says before kissing her again.

"I am cold, freezing. Let's get out of here," Liz suddenly suggests. Like lightning she is on her feet, grabbing the torch.

"I don't want to come here again. It's too scary," she exclaims firmly, taking her lover's polo shirt off and putting her tiny bikini back on.

Secretly I am heaving a sigh of relief. I can't hold out much longer either.

"Of course, I understand," Max replies hesitantly before blowing out the candles.

"Where have you parked your car?" Liz asks urgently.

"Lance has got the car today. I have walked down," Max tells her. Then he adds, "I've got about an hour until Louisa comes home from golf."

As quickly as the couple have arrived they are leaving. Aided by Max's powerful torch they head back out of the church. My body feels like frozen stiff but at least I can climb out of my hiding place now. It is completely dark again in the church. From memory I can find my way to where Max had lit the candles. There is not much left of them. Grateful to have finally found some matches I use the candle light to guide me out of the hall. This was the worst experience of my life and I vow never to return to the church, ever.

Very carefully I enter the passageway that leads to the exit. I have to ensure that Max and Liz have left before moving on. As slowly as I can I proceed through the damp tunnel, guarding the valuable flame with one hand and holding on to the leaking rock with the other. If Petroc ever found out what I have witnessed here today he would want to kill those two. I must do everything in my power to keep this secret, to save Petroc from the truth, the pain.

It is not until I park my bicycle in the backyard of my grandparents' house that I realise what has happened to me. These last couple of hours have not been a nightmare, a very bad dream while asleep on the beach. The wounds are real. My right flip-flop is covered in dried blood, my toe showing a deep cut and several minor scratches. I have also got blood on my fingers.

How can I get into the house without being questioned? I need a shower, a plaster and a stiff drink. Leaning on my bike I can hear a commotion in the garden next door. It's no good. I don't want to be seen like this.

As fast as I can I enter the house, shoot up the stairs to the bathroom.

"Jenny, dear, is everything alright?" I hear Gran's voice from downstairs.

"Yes, yes," I reply but I don't believe that she can hear me.

My head already under the water of the nice warm shower I take a deep breath. Okay, I have been climbing around the rocks and I slipped, hurt myself. It's nothing serious, just a few cuts. Yes, that is what I will tell them when I go downstairs later. Standing under the fast running water I am haunted by what I have witnessed. How can I ever face Max again when he comes to the fence and offers me a beer? How can I ever forget his naked body in the candle light? And poor Louisa – does she have any idea what's going on behind her back? And Petroc? He is suspecting his best friend of cheating but Lance is innocent, totally innocent, the honourable Sir Lancelot! He was on the same beach with his girlfriend when his dad... Oh, I don't want to be reminded of it.

I have no idea how long I have been under the shower but I can expect a big telling-off from my grandad. He has a little gadget, his favourite one, supplied by a national energy company that advises him exactly on how much gas, electricity and water has been used in house and garden. Well, I'd better prepare myself for a pay cut due to rising water bills whilst I am here.

Anyway, I feel an awful lot better when I arrive downstairs to perform my little act that I have rehearsed so thoroughly under the shower.

"You should know better than climbing around those dangerous rocks at your age," criticises Gran.

I nod ruefully.

"Not to worry, I have not come to any harm," I reply softly. If only my grandparents knew what I have been through this afternoon. It will take me forever to get over that picture in my mind.

My appetite is not good tonight either, giving my caring grandparents even more reason for concern. It is not until I help Gran with the dishes after dinner that she speaks to me in private.

"Richard has been down to the pub earlier. A friend of Mary's knows next door. You may be interested to know that Max is actually Cornish. He was born in St Ives and he grew up here before moving up-country to study. After he married Louisa they moved back for a while to raise a family," she reports.

"I see," I comment dreamily. And there it is again, so clear in my mind's eye, that picture of Max and Liz, the screaming. I feel sick, properly nauseous. Surely, I won't be physically ill now?

Leaving a half-dry frying pan and the tea towel behind I escape the kitchen, make my way upstairs to the toilet. In the safety of the bathroom my stomach is still cramping but the ill feeling passes over as quickly as it appeared. I fill my tooth beaker with water, drink the contents in one sip and return downstairs.

Gran has finished off the dishes. She says I look pale and Grandad advises me to have an early night.

Obediently I go back upstairs to my room. I cannot resist looking out of the window into next door's garden. Luckily, no one is outside tonight.

I manage to stay in bed until around 10 pm. Then I cannot stand it any longer. I want to go down to the beach, meet Petroc. Never before have I felt such an urge to see someone. Something inside me has changed. It is so powerful, like a calling. God is telling me to go, I chuckle. I put my jeans on and a hoody and go downstairs.

"I'll go for a little ride, get some fresh air," I tell Grandad who is sitting in front of the TV. Gran has gone to the WI tonight.

"What? This time of day? You haven't been well," Grandad reminds me.

"I need to get out. Please don't worry, I am a big girl now, old enough to make my own decisions. See you in the morning," I say quickly and leave the house.

As fast as my legs will allow it I cycle down to the beach. Of course, there is no guarantee that Petroc will be at the church tonight but I am prepared to take that risk. I decide to park my bike in a slightly different position than usual. Then I run across the dunes towards the secret rock. It is late, getting darker by the minute. I must hurry to get to the church. On a mild summer's evening like this many walkers are still about. Nervously I check all around me. Thinking carefully about how to best approach the rocks I spot a dark figure jogging towards me. I recognise the runner's black tracksuit bottoms and loose fitting hoody immediately.

"Hi," Petroc greets me, totally out of breath.

"I was hoping you would be coming," he admits, seeming relieved.

"I wasn't but…" I start and Petroc completes my sentence, "God was telling me to come."

"Yes," I say, not smiling.

I can see that Petroc is even more nervous than I am. The expression on his ashen face gives his deepest feelings away.

"What's up?" I ask him.

"Someone has been in the church," he explains angrily.

"That's why I came tonight. It was me," I say quickly. The oversized black hood is framing the talented musician's pale face as he frowns. I can see that he does not believe me.

"I was here this afternoon. I wanted to leave you a message," I desperately try to explain.

"What message?" he asks, his eyes scanning the long beach for people.

"I wanted to put something right," I continue, bowing my head.

"Why didn't you before?" he enquires urgently, standing close to me but not touching me.

"I lied to you the other night," I confess bravely.

"I know but why did you have to leave the church in such a mess?" he asks instantly.

"I couldn't find the lighter, it was so dark, I am so sorry," I stutter helplessly.

"Listen, why can't you stop lying to me? Someone has been in my church and it was not just you!" he says sharply, his voice raised.

"I can prove to you that it was only me," I argue.

"Impossible but okay, go ahead!" he demands immediately. His tone does not sound friendly at all.

"Let's go inside and I'll show you something," I suggest, looking out across the bay as darkness sets in. Will I be able to face this cave again, after all that has happened earlier?

Without further ado Petroc turns on his heels and leads me to the high cliffs. I can sense that he is absolutely furious. I don't know why but he sends me into the narrow gap first. Once we are far enough inside the tunnel he whispers, "Right, show me how you got on without a lighter!"

I find it difficult, too daunting.

"See, you can't do it. Nobody can without this," he says from behind me, removing a lighter from the pocket of his jogging bottoms.

"I was here this afternoon, I swear," I tell him in the passageway. As we approach the actual church I take a deep breath.

"I really am sorry for turning up the sand in here, using most of the candles, the matches..." I explain.

Petroc who now magically produces a torch points to the spot where I have hurt myself.

"There is blood," he states the obvious.

"Yes, I injured my foot. I could not see well enough. It was foolish. Look, I can show you," I reply. With that I bend down to remove my trainers and socks.

"Don't bother – who else was here?" he asks then, the light of his torch examining the sand for footprints.

"No one, just me," I lie, trying to remain strong.

Suddenly Petroc grabs me, his slim hands squeezing my arms hard. Once again I am afraid of him, more than ever.

"This is a place of trust, remember? You are not telling the truth. You can't fool me. Someone else was here today," he insists, his grip really hurting me now.

"Nobody else was here while I was," I lie, despite the watchful eye of Jesus on the cross in front of me. Deep inside I am asking for forgiveness already.

Petroc lets me go.

"Well, in that case someone must have come here after you left," he deducts nervously.

Angrily he points his torch at me.

"How can you be so stupid? If you come here at daytime people will see you, follow you, wonder where you have gone, search for the entrance – holidaymakers with torches, just like this one. That's no way to keep a secret. I cannot believe you did this to me," he shouts, his voice echoing off the walls in the great hall.

"I made sure nobody saw me, Petroc. I did take care," I defend myself from his attack.

"Nothing like this has happened before – until I met you," he says then, almost in tears.

Suddenly he sounds weak, the anger turning to sadness.

"But, Petroc, there was always a chance, wasn't there? How could you ever be sure that nobody will find this cave? You found it, so why shouldn't anyone else?" I tell him.

He is still clutching his torch, making no attempt to light any candles. I am no longer scared as I put my hand on his bony shoulder. Like a child he starts crying, weeping. I have never seen or heard a grown man sob like this.

"It's all my fault and I am sorry, very, very sorry," I say, trying to comfort him.

Slowly he drops his torch into the sand, embracing me with all his might. His hooded head is resting on my shoulder.

"You don't understand what this church means to me," he whispers then, still shedding tears. I feel his warm lips kissing my neck, his hands stroking my back. Although I still don't know what to make of him I am enjoying his touch. Anything Petroc does feels so different, so out of the ordinary, just like his music. He is inexplicably sensual, sexy.

"Why don't you try and explain, talk about it. It may help," I suggest carefully.

Petroc pulls me over to one of his wooden trunks. For a moment we sit down in silence. It appears that the batteries in his torch are fading. The light is no longer bright. I am holding his cold hands in mine, torn between telling all and just listening to him. Several minutes pass with Petroc simply refusing to start a conversation.

"I came here to tell you that I am known as Jen, not Sue. Susan is my middle name. I came to leave you a message, admitting that I lied to you," I begin slowly.

"At the *Sandsifter* I heard your friend calling you Jen. I knew then that you've lied to me," he responds disappointedly.

"That new song of yours, *Candle Light*, it is good, very good. You performed it so beautifully. Everyone was impressed," I tell him admiringly, hoping to change the subject.

"I played it for you once I knew you were there. I wanted to talk to you, " he replies, cuddling into me.

As my fingers touch his troubled-looking face, in readiness to finally take down his black hood, the batteries of the torch totally expire. The church is left in complete darkness but despite it all my fear of him has subsided. My hands are holding on to Petroc's slim body, my lips desperately seeking his. For the first time we are kissing freely, without any doubts. What is this man doing to me? Or is it this place?

"Have you ever stayed here overnight?" I ask him.

"No, it is too dangerous. I never stay longer than two or three hours. The air down here is thin. I don't trust it," he answers.

"Then it will soon be time for us to leave," I guess and I add: "Before we go, will you play that song for me again, please?"

In the pitch dark I cannot see the expression on Petroc's face but his reply sounds incredibly sad, "I can't play here anymore. It's over. The church has been contaminated with an evil spirit. Someone has trodden on this holy ground, without permission and that makes the church obsolete – for good. This will be the last time I've spent time in here. The secret is out."

I shake my head.

"But you can't do that! Whoever came here may never come again. Where will you go to be inspired, where will you write your music?" I exclaim, remaining firmly in Petroc's arms.

"Don't try and stop me, Jen. There is a reason why this was a secret place. You don't understand," he says, releasing himself from my embrace in order to find spare batteries for his torch.

"What if you ever found out who was here today?" I challenge him as he struggles to replace the batteries in the dark.

"It makes no difference to the necessity of closure. There's some history to this church," he says and somehow he manages to make his torch work again.

As so many times before he hides away any remaining matchboxes and candles but tonight he takes the crucifix off the back wall and drops it carefully into the cool sand.

"Tomorrow night I will come here to clear this place out. Will you help me?" he asks then.

I hesitate as I am not prepared to commit to an answer. Leaning against the damp cold rock I enquire, "When did you find this cave?"

"A very long time ago. Come on, we must leave now. I don't want to talk about it," he says, clearly trying to avoid a painful answer.

With his torch pointing towards the exit he urges me to get out.

In silence we walk back along the dark beach to the car park. We are not touching.

"I insist on driving you home, no argument. It's well after midnight," Petroc says kindly.

I am wondering where his car is as there is no old red Fiesta in the car park, in fact there aren't any cars left at all.

In the slight summer night's breeze we stroll past my bicycle and along the road that leads to the headland overlooking the famous lighthouse. Soon Petroc's torch is pointing at a white Audi that has been squeezed into the dunes by the roadside.

"My mum's car," he explains. All of a sudden I feel tired, shattered.

We do not speak on the way back to my grandparents' home. Although I am exhausted I am eager to observe his facial expression when I tell him to stop the car next door to *Seabreeze*. Surely it must hurt, the memory of the barbeque, that fateful night. Will he say anything, mention Lance? He doesn't. He is a professional performer, an actor, good at hiding true feelings, keeping secrets. All about him seems totally in control, wide awake. As if nothing has ever happened he pulls up at Grandad's drive, a footstep away from Max's large property.

"Good night," he simply says, not trying to kiss me.

"Night, night," I reply a little disappointedly.

"Pray for us," he adds, and with that I get out of the car and he drives off.

The next morning I am being woken by the horrendous noise the builders make next door. It is a kind of drilling, very high-pitched, hard to describe. Some of the vibrations are strong enough to make my room shake. From downstairs I can hear Grandad cursing, swearing. Smiling to myself I stretch. I feel surprisingly good, quite relaxed after a good night's sleep. Strangely enough I did not dream of Max and Liz, nor Petroc – and I also failed to pray!

On tiptoes I walk over to the window. The sun is shining but there are plenty of thick white clouds in the sky as well. Apart from a couple of men in hard hats, dirty shorts and workman's boots I spot two women in the garden next door – Louisa, in jeans and polo shirt and a younger woman, dressed in a fluorescent green vest top and black, skin-tight, knee-long leggings and trainers. Her hair is tied back and I cannot be sure but she could well be the super lucky woman who seems to be Lance's girlfriend. Sighing I turn way. Time is ticking on. I have to get ready for work, open the car park. Before I leave my vantage place by the window I watch the two women talking to the builders, the younger one using her slim, tanned arms to demonstrate the size of something. Then I hear my Gran calling me for breakfast.

Grandad is trying to read his morning paper. He opens his mouth in an attempt to say something but the building noise makes any kind of conversation in this house impossible. "I am going to have words with him next door again," he suddenly shouts across the table. "I want to know what they are planning to do over there before they apply for permission from the Council," he continues, slamming the paper onto the empty plate in front of him. I don't know what he has been reading but on the page opposite is the photograph taken at the *Sandsifter* showing the pretty Liz pulling an angry-looking Petroc onto the dance floor.

"All over?" is the emboldened headline.

"Can I have that for a moment, please?" I ask, my hands already reaching out for the newspaper. If Grandad's looks could kill I wouldn't be around anymore to read the article but he does not say anything as I fold the paper so that I can quickly scan the contents of the short write-up. Not surprisingly there is speculation that the relationship of "Monopoly's" front man and the "millionaire's daughter from Falmouth" has turned sour. "According to a source close to the couple there are no wedding bells on the horizon" I read. The remaining sentences deal with the new song which has already been tipped to hit the national charts and propel Monopoly into proper stardom.

Swallowing hard I put the paper down.

"Have you heard of him?" Gran suddenly asks, pointing at Petroc in the photograph. I nod eagerly.

"They have been talking about him in the pub the other day," Grandad interjects.

"What did they say?" I want to know, blushing.

"They said he is local, a great talent, on his way to becoming a famous international rock star. Some people in the village have seen him on the beach down here," Gran explains.

"He's parked his car in our car park once or twice – our claim to fame!" I reply quickly, looking down onto my plate.

"Well, I wouldn't recognise a chap like that but then, I am old. His music is not for us. Better fit they'd sent Tom Jones here on holiday!" Grandad comments.

I smile mildly and I cannot help adding, "He's good, really great. Let's hope he'll make it." With that I get up, just remembering that my bike is still down at the car park.

Naturally, I am very late this morning, having to walk to the beach. It is not quite eight o'clock yet but to get there on time I would need to run. Knowing that there is not much point bursting any blood vessels I stroll happily along the narrow road.

"I'm not in love," I am singing to myself, hopping and skipping like a young foal. Totally oblivious to the traffic behind me I take up most of the road. I do not even notice a car pulling up right next to me.

"Can I give you a lift?" a friendly voice asks me.

The words send shock waves through my entire body – it's Sir Lancelot in his father's Mercedes, on his own!

"That's very kind of you, thanks," I accept nervously.

"A good turn deserves another. I really appreciated not being charged for parking yesterday," Lance says as I climb into the luxury car.

"It's a pleasure," I reply.

Oh, yes, it is a pleasure sitting in such a nice car next to such an attractive man. It is just a pity that the way down to the beach only takes a few minutes at Lance's speed. He drops me at the barrier, I let him in, and off paying again, and then I watch him walking across the dunes. Where is he going this early in the morning, I wonder?

Unlocking my hut I am trying to recover from the journey down here.

"He really is lovely," I whisper dreamily.

For his sake I am hoping that he has his mother's genes and not those of his good-looking but dishonest father. Being a cheat is a horrible thing...

"Here, looks like you've got a chance after all," a very familiar voice shouts at me. No doubt the words are meant to be loud enough to wake me from my wildest daydreams. It's Tina, the window of her car wound right down, and she is waving the local newspaper in the air.

"Good morning, and thanks, I've read it," I reply casually.

"Well, sounds like he's a good catch – on his way to worldwide fame, aye!" Tina sneers nastily and puts her foot down. She is not asking for my permission but she takes the best space in the car park.

"Five pounds, please," I call after her but she just laughs.

Watching her locking the car and walking over to the café I almost miss the next customer queuing up. I am really not with it this morning. It's a white Audi, including cool surfer-type driver; woolly hat – although it is a resonably warm summer's day – shades and a grey tracksuit top, done up to the neck.

"How long has that Merc been here?" he asks when I eventually wake up.

"Petroc!" I exclaim happily.

He hands me a five-pound note.

"Answer my question – how long?" he demands rudely.

"I don't know, five minutes perhaps," I reply hesitantly.

Leaving a huge cloud of dust behind him, Petroc steps on the accelerator. He deliberately brakes hard, close to the shiny Mercedes, so that the luxury car gets covered in sand. My brain is finally starting to get into gear. Is Petroc suspecting his best friend of visiting his church?

In the not too far distance, at the other end of my car park, I can see him jumping out of the car, slamming the driver's door shut. Without any reference to me he storms off, running across the dunes. My heart beating like a drum I decide that I must intervene before disaster strikes. As fast as I can I pull my mobile phone out of my pocket, pressing the special button for Tina's number.

"Come on, answer it, now, I know you are in there," I shout at the phone, looking over to the café at the same time.

It seems like an age until she finally responds.

"You must help me out, Tina, be a good friend. Please, can you take over the car park for 15 minutes? I need to see someone on the beach. It's urgent, please!" I shout into the phone, my voice full of panic.

"Okay, okay, I am coming, dear," Tina says. Seconds later she jogs across the car park.

Already on my way to the dunes I throw the heavy bag with the change in it over to her and run off. Charging through the deep sand I am ploughing forward. This early in the day there are not many people on the beach but I cannot see any signs of Petroc. Feeling anxious and terribly unfit I have to stop for a moment to catch my breath. As I look further down along the still deserted beach I can make two figures out in the distance, up to their waists in the sea, fighting. Running as fast as I can I make my way to the scene. Petroc is fully dressed, Lance in just his swimming trunks. With high waves rolling in the men are struggling to stand up and exchange blows. "Stop!" I shout as I get closer.

"Stop, stop or I will call the lifeguards," I scream nervously.

Petroc, preparing to throw another punch, loses his footing and the fighting ceases momentarily.

"Don't hit him, please stop. It's not him you are looking for," I call out angrily.

Just as I reach the shoreline where the two men are fighting another person arrives from the opposite side of the beach.

"What's going on here?" a female voice is asking.

Only now I take notice, look up. The fluorescent green vest top is wet through and I recognise the woman immediately. Relentlessly breaking waves are hitting the shore as the tide is coming in further. Suddenly all four of us are in the water. The men look cold, shivering. My heart goes out to the handsome Lance whose normally so perfect nose is bleeding heavily. Petroc, his woolly hat partly pulled off his head and the stylish sunglasses broken, walks out of the sea.

"What do you know about it?" he asks me, sounding very unkind.

Lance's girlfriend says nothing as he follows us onto dry land. She is still recovering from her morning run.

"Everything. I know who you should be after – and it's not Lance," I reply, not realising that I have never been formally introduced to my grandparents' neighbour and therefore should probaly not call him by his Christian name.

"Can someone tell me what this is all about?" Lance's girlfriend is asking.

In her wet trainers she is jogging up and down on the spot to keep herself warm. Noisy seagulls are circling overhead as the mighty waves continue crashing onto the beach. Why does she not help Lance, touch him, comfort him? He is shaking, from head to toe.

"It's alright, Tammy, just some unfinished business," Petroc says, taking his wet tracksuit top off and offering it to Lance.

"Keep it," the gorgeous but badly bleeding Sir Lancelot responds, throwing the garment back to his friend.

"Anyway, who are you?" Tammy enquires coolly, her brown eyes assessing me arrogantly.

As I look at her more closely I can see a resemblance.

"I'm a neighbour..." I utter carefully.

"Her grandparents live next door to your mum and dad," Petroc clarifies the situation.

While he is fiddling nervously with his broken shades I feel like sinking deep into the sand. Now I get it – Tammy is Lance's sister!

Both men, cold and wet and fresh from their fight, look injured. With water and blood running down his handsome face poor Lance is in a real mess. Tammy, still irritatingly jumping up and down, is shaking her head.

"See you guys later then," she says and off she runs, water splashing, along the beach.

It appears that she is not the slightest bit worried about her brother.

The morning sun is peering through the thick clouds for just a few seconds providing a little warmth for the wet men. I feel helpless but eventually I pull my last clean tissue out of my shorts.

"Here you are," I say softly, wishing I could touch the now not so lovely-looking Lance.

Without a further word to either of us Petroc decides to walk on ahead, leaving me with his friend. Carefully Lance wipes his paining nose, and then he marches towards the spot where his clothes are neatly folded up on a black beach towel.

"You need to be cleaned up properly," I say to him, stating the obvious.

Secretly I am admiring his broad shoulders and slim hips. He's so attractive, even now. Following him and staying by his side I ask, "Does your nose hurt much?"

"No, I'll survive," he responds heroically, rubbing his beach towel around his throbbing face.

Then I pluck up all my courage.

"This should never have happened..." I start, sighing.

"Thanks for your help anyway," he says, slowly starting to get dressed.

I feel like a spare part, unwanted. The brave Sir Lancelot is not interested in me. If only he knew how much I fancy him, even with that bleeding nose! My head tells me to leave him alone but my heart realises that this is a brilliant chance, perhaps the only one I'll ever have to get closer to him.

"Did you know that Liz is having an affair?" I ask, taking a very deep breath.

His warm brown eyes look serious as he answers, "Not until Petroc almost killed me!" In the distance I can see Lance's attacker rapidly approaching the car park.

As more and more clouds gather in the sky above us the temperature is dropping considerably. In my mind I have hundreds of questions that I want to ask Lance but I am not feeling confident.

"They've got a first aid kit at the lifeguard hut," I say, pointing over to the wooden shed in the dunes.

"Thank you but I am sure I will be fine once I get home and clean myself up," Lance replies.

He is walking fast next to me now. Much too soon we are back in the car park.

Tina is looking out for me. I can see that she is eyeing up the man in my company. As Lance reaches the safety of the Mercedes she catches up with me.

"What's happened to him?" she enquires curiously.

"Bit of an accident," I reply, trying to make light of the situation.

"Accident or fight?" Tina asks immediately.

Her question surprises me.

"The latter," I admit.

Tina nods.

"Thought so. I have seen a very livid person leaving the car park a few minutes ago – and am pretty sure it was Petroc Hayman," she says.

"You are right," I tell her but I don't want to go into any details.

"Interesting. So, who is that guy with the Merc?" Tina asks.

"He's the son of Grandad's new neighbours and Petroc's best friend," I respond as Tina starts laughing.

"Fine way to treat your best friend, don't you agree?" she chuckles.

Sighing I shake my head. It suddenly dawns on Tina what my words mean.

"I don't believe it! Are you telling me you've actually met Petroc Hayman, I mean properly? When, where? Oh, Jen, you must tell me all about that. What's he like when he doesn't bash other people's noses in?"

Making up a story to Tina feels almost worse than lying to Petroc. I am not used to such a secretive life. This summer has turned out to be so different from any others before. Nothing is quite like it was in previous years. I have come here to get away from my busy life in London, to enjoy myself and to escape the frustration of fancying someone I cannot have – and what happens? Things are turning out just as complicated here as they are at home!

As evening breaks I make a conscious decision not to go down to the beach. My mission has been accomplished. All I've wanted was meet Lance. Frankly, it could have been in happier circumstances, but anyway, I've met him now. For me a relationship with someone like Petroc Hayman is out of the question. He will soon move into higher circles, travel the world, perform in amazing places with millions of fans following his every step. No doubt he will always take up a special place in my heart but I have decided that he is not for me.

And Lance? I don't know what to think of him really. He is a fantastic-looking man, much like his dad, but at this moment in time both father and son put me off. Max is a womaniser and his son a bit too aloof to be fun to be with. All in all they are a bit of a disappointment those people from next door. Louisa seems a genuinely nice person, though her daughter appears a lot less warm and friendly. During that brief encounter on the beach I did not take to her at all.

A hectic bank holiday weekend at the car park goes by but I hear and see nothing of Petroc or the next door neighbours. It is not until Tina tells me the latest news that I start worrying. Monopoly have cancelled all further engagements. According to local newspaper reports lead singer Petroc Hayman is unwell and needs some time out.

"I am surprised you didn't know about this," Tina says as we are sitting in her tiny front room.

I am having a day off from my car park duties today because the weather is terrible.

"God is punishing him for hurting Lance," I whisper.

"What did you just say?" asks Tina, frowning and jumping up from her creaking settee.

"Nothing, just a silly remark," I reply casually.

Luckily Tina believes me but she senses that I am suddenly very concerned about Petroc.

"You really like him, don't you?" she says passing me a hot cup of tea.

"Don't you have any means of contacting him?" she wants to know.

"Yes, I have. All I need to do is go next door. Lance will know how to get in touch with him," I answer.

Only a week ago the prospect of ringing the doorbell at *Seabreeze* would have excited me no end. I was looking for nothing but a reason to go there and now I am not so keen anymore.

Still, on this atrocious Tuesday evening, I decide to go next door before returning to my grandparents. Less nervous than I used to be I walk up the newly laid drive. I notice that the Mercedes is not there. Trying to shelter from the continuous rain I am almost running as I approach the massive modern front door. Shaking the water off my rain jacket I press the doorbell.

Somehow I get the impression that nobody is in. Just as I am about to leave again Louisa comes to the door.

"Hi," I say as cheerfully as I can.

"Is Lance in, please?" I ask.

It does not take a detective to find out that Louisa is not looking happy.

"He left at the weekend. He's back at work," she says.

"Could you give me his mobile phone number, please? I'd like to speak to him," I request urgently, wondering if Louisa might have been crying before I arrived.

"Yes, of course, do come in," she finally offers.

Quite a lot of progress has been made inside the house. The new interior is very luxurious, most tasteful, all in keeping with the grandeur of the old house. Immediately I spot framed photographs of Lance and Tammy that catch my eye. They must have been sporty children: There is Lance as a teenager with an enormous golf trophy and Tammy, in her picture a little older, running. For minutes I stare at them as Louisa writes down Lance's number. She continues to look very strained. I am so tempted to say something, to ask her if she is alright but it is none of my business so I decide not to.

"Thank you," is all that I utter, ready to leave.

"My pleasure. Please tell your grandparents that they will have a bit of peace and quiet for a while. We are putting our works on hold for a few weeks," Louisa tells me.

I am expecting some further explanation but it does not come. Deep inside I am concerned about the situation but what can I do? Pulling my hood over my head I run down the empty drive and across to my grandparents' house.

Later this evening the rain is still absolutely lashing down. This is the worst I have seen it all summer. Grandad has been invited to join a quiz team at the pub so he is prepared to venture out but Gran has called her "Village Over 60s Club" off.

"Nobody will be out and about in this weather," she justifies her decision to cancel.

At dinner time I tell her about Louisa's message.

"I am glad that you have spoken to her. She hasn't been outside for days. I was starting to wonder if she is not well," Gran says kindly.

The temptation to discuss my observations with Gran is strong but then I resolve not to. Instead I go upstairs. No point looking out of the window. Lance is no longer around. Apart from huge raindrops and a thoroughly black sky, there is nothing to see. Hesitantly I pick up my mobile phone from the bedside table. Should I ring him? Send him a text? Just ask him for Petroc's number? In the end I do nothing. Why am I worrying about him? He does not need me. If he believes in a higher power then I am of no help to him – and still, I feel responsible for the closure of his church, guilty. If he is unable to perform now, is it all my fault? Suddenly I am plagued by a bad conscience, and not just that: I am seriously concerned about him, his mental and physical well-being.

Instead of using my phone to ring Lance I am sitting on my bed testing the torch function on it. Would it provide sufficient light for me to enter the church? I don't even know if Grandad has a larger working torch anywhere around the house or in his garden shed. Perhaps I could pinch a handful of Gran's emergency candles that she keeps in the kitchen cupboard and some matches. Checking the time I decide that I must leave the house before Grandad returns from the pub. They still observe the "last orders" rule in the village and on week nights the bar closes around 10:30 pm. Gran is normally in the bed by then. The last thing I want is to be caught. I certainly don't wish to explain to my grandparents why I am off to the beach at this time of night. If Petroc is not in the church I will be back before midnight in any case.

Sneaking very quietly downstairs, putting my rain jacket on and helping myself to a brand new box of matches and a couple of white candles from the kitchen I leave the house. It is too dangerous to take the bike out of the garden shed and through the creaking back gate. As spooky as it may feel in the dark I must take the risk and walk.

It is still raining but not as heavily as earlier on. My heart racing I jog down the road. In the distance I can make out the dunes, the sea and the flashing light of Godrevy Lighthouse. Under the very few street lights that guide my way the fine rain is driving across the open countryside. What a truly foul night! All looks black, sad and hopeless. How different this place is when the sun shines! Not a single car has passed me on the road down to the car park tonight. Who wants to be on the beach on a night like this? I am almost there now, sweat building up inside my waterproof jacket. I've made good time. As if my life depends on it I run across the empty car park, through the dunes and along the steep cliffs. The beach is completely deserted, the tide out. No need to check for walkers at this late hour. In the rain the sand feels heavy, large lumps of it sticking to my shoes. I continue running, for once knowing exactly where I am heading. By now I have learnt to recognise the rock face, the enormous walls that hide the gap, the entrance to Petroc's church. With a mixture of fear and excitement I put my mobile phone into torch mode and enter the tunnel. Why do I find my way so easily tonight? In next to no time I reach the higher part of the passage way, then the large hall. Although I have prepared myself for it I cannot really believe it until now. The church has gone. There is absolutely nothing left of Petroc's belongings, no boxes, no keyboard, no candles, no matches, no crucifix. It is shocking, staggering. Anyone who has not seen the church would never believe that there was one here, ever.

With sadness in my heart I bend down to touch the once so holy sand. It's over, the church and Petroc. Why did I believe I would meet him here on a horrendous night like tonight? Maybe he is tucked up warm in his bed somewhere or maybe he is back rehearsing, writing new songs, his beloved music. I take one last look at this rather ordinary-looking cave, the secret chamber that only days ago was Petroc's church. Almost lovingly I touch the rugged walls. This once so awe-inspiring hall is reduced to nothing but damp and cold granite. After a moment of hesitation I sink to my knees, my jeans instantly soaking up the moisture from the sand. I bow my head and pray, something I cannot remember ever doing before in my life. My eyes closed I kneel there until my tears flow freely. I weep and I sob, just like Petroc had done when he realised that an evil spirit had taken over this sacred place. Suddenly I lose all awareness of my surroundings, I am transported onto a different planet, to outer space, to the abyss and I feel a hand touching my shoulder, very gently. I do not react. Surely this dreamlike experience will pass but the bright light that surrounds me does not come from the flashlight on my tiny mobile phone. The cave is alight as I open my teary eyes and the grip on my shoulder feels stronger.

"You've lied to me, Jen. You keep doing it. You've done it from the start," I hear a voice say.

The words are spoken so clearly. Utterly terrified I turn around. The light has disappeared and there is nobody else in the cave, just me. My fingers clutching my mobile phone I get up. I am shaking, freezing.

"Petroc!" I shout desperately, the echo repeating his name several times before it goes quiet.

In a state of trance, of total confusion, I creep on all fours towards the exit. Having reached the narrowest part of the tunnel it remains pitch dark. I am too stunned to catch up with reality. In panic and desperation I look all around me. I've been here before, many times now. This passageway must end soon. I must surely be close enough to see the gap, the point where a fraction of natural light is visible, the entrance and exit, but there is nothing, nothing but solid rock. Shining my dim flashlight all around me the passage seems black and endless to either side, the same going forward as back. Breathing rapidly I realise that I am trapped. There is no light at the end of the tunnel. What was the only way in and out of here half an hour ago has been blocked. Someone has moved a large boulder into the gap, the only means of escape. Trying to come to my senses I tell myself to think clearly. Examining the rock I am able to establish how large the massive stone is that has been put into the void. After a while I can detect a slither of natural light, or to be more precise, darkness. With all the power that I have left in my body I try and push the rock out of the way. It is moving in the wet sand, ever so slightly. Through the tiny slit I can see that it is still raining. Again, I push but my strength is fading, as is the light my mobile phone has provided me with all evening.

Overcome by a terrifying panic I scream, I shout for help. Knowing that I cannot expect anyone to be around in the middle of the night I start to cry. Whoever has locked me in this prison could not have realised that I am in here. Nobody even knows that I have left my grandparents' house. They must think I am in bed, sleeping. Nobody will look for me until perhaps the morning...

It is so cold in the depth of the dark rocks. In all my desperation I am trying to revive my phone but apart from the fact that there is no signal down in the belly of the cliffs the battery has given up its ghost. In my pocket I still have two unused candles and one box of matches. Realising that I will have to be very economical with any source of light and heat in order to survive until the morning, I plant the first candle into the sand in front of me. What is the point in worrying until then? I must save my energy for another push for freedom and hang on, simply wait until daylight.

Surprised by my strange feeling of courage, I light the candle. My watch tells me that it is just after midnight. It will be a very long night. For a second time I get into position to push, careful not to disturb the candle. Frightened and exhausted I notice that I have been successful. Again, the heavy rock has moved a fraction. If I keep going all night I might just get out by early morning. The exercise is keeping me warm as I attempt to push some more. My feeble efforts have finally created a gap as wide as my arm. Through it I can make out the beach, the black sky and the rain. My ear close to the boulder I can clearly hear the powerful sound of the sea, large waves crashing onto the shore. I am living in hope and therefore I push again. This time the rock does not move. Accepting that I must have reached the point of exhaustion I sit down, next to my candle.

Staring at the flickering flame I bow my head. How could I ever have got myself in this crazy situation? What is it about this cave? It is unnerving to think that it is something special, supernatural. As I look up I see a hand, a wet, pale, slim, very familiar hand touching the dark boulder through the gap.

"Petroc!" I shout once again, louder and more desperately than ever, my hand reaching for his.

The relief I feel in my entire body is overwhelming. Squeezing his soft fingers tightly I beg, "Get me out of here, please!"

Admiring his strength I watch him get to work on the rock. Within seconds my candle is extinguished by a strong draught, and Petroc manages to move the massive boulder far enough to one side for me to climb out. I have never been as happy as in this moment. All I want is embrace my saviour, hold him tight, thank him for releasing me from this horrifying chamber but he is pushing me off, refusing to be touched. His black clothing is wet through and sticking to his skin.

"Hang on, Jen. You've got some explaining to do," he says and his voice does not sound kind at all.

"I will but not here, please," I reply, shivering.

"Oh, yes, here, in there and now," he insists.

Why is there no let-up in the heavy rain? The cloudy sky above seems so terribly dark, but I can clearly see that Petroc is pointing to the entrance of the cave.

"In here and no more lies!" he demands angrily.

His mannerism frightens me but once again I am trying to convince myself that I am not afraid of him anymore. Obediently I return to the inside of the tunnel, followed by him and his bright torch. Together we creep back into the empty great hall.

"Okay, I am listening. What happened here that afternoon when you came at daytime?" he asks firmly. He is standing in front of me, not touching me, the torch directed onto my worried face. I sigh, take a deep breath, pause for a second, but then I let it all out, the truth and nothing but the truth.

Towards the end of my lengthy confession I sink to the ground, shaking my head and covering my face with both hands. While I have been talking Petroc has remained stone-faced, not a single muscle is moving in his body. His eyes simply stare at me in disbelief. It's a most peculiar reaction to my perfectly true but upsetting story. Suddenly I feel the need to elaborate, go into every fine detail that I can recall from that awful afternoon but still there is no expression in Petroc's steely blue eyes and the pale, thin face. It's like an empty space, frozen.

"When I saw you hitting Lance I wanted to tell you that you were wrong to hurt him like that," I eventually end my monologue.

Feeling rather exhausted and a little dizzy I am getting ready to rise from the coarse sand.

"Sit down!" Petroc demands strictly, continuing to point the bright beam of his torch into my eyes.

Doubtfully I assess the cold, damp sand but I dare not disobey. Silently I drop down again, trying not to take my eyes off him. Then he sits down beside me, putting his wet and cold arm around my shoulders.

"It has happened before, Jen," he starts and everything about him is changing, his voice, his body language, his facial expression.

He places his torch in front of us, into the dark sand, his right arm pulling me tighter towards him, his left hand taking my right. "On this very day, exactly 19 years ago, we found this cave," he declares sincerely. He can hardly speak, so emotional he feels right now.

"A beautiful, bright summer's day – a Sunday. We were all on the beach – my gran, my mum, my little brother, only two years old at the time, and Max and Louisa, Lance and Tammy. My dad had to work as so often at the weekends. Play was getting a bit boring and Lance and I went off exploring. I had just turned six, Lance was still five. Tammy had been entrusted to look after us but she was only seven years old herself and more interested in girly things, I suppose. We ran around the rocks, played hide and seek and then I came across this little ridge. I hid, deeper and deeper in the tunnel, until I got so frightened that I called for help. Luckily Lance heard me."

As Petroc takes a deep breath I notice that he is starting to shake violently. Despite it all, his arm and hands feel strangely warm all of a sudden and he is continuing to stroke me lovingly.

"He heard me and I asked him to join me in the tunnel," he continues, "We were fascinated, very brave for young boys. In the dark we crept on and on until it became all too frightening, too impossible. We made a pact to return with torches, explore properly next time."

I open my mouth, wanting to make a comment but Petroc signals me not to interrupt him.

"We did not manage to return, not as soon as we wanted to anyway. We were best friends, met up daily after school, always discussing the cave and keeping it a secret but the most frustrating problem was that our families would not go to the beach again for some time so we had no chance of realising our plans. Amazingly we did not give up. Then, one day, my mum took my brother to my gran's and me to Lance's house. She did that now and again to have some time to herself. My dad was always away working, being a miner it was hard and irregular work. Max tended not be around on those occasions either and Tammy, being that little bit older, was often allowed to visit her friends. Anyway, one day, after much begging, Louisa took us two boys to the beach. It was another fantastically hot and beautiful day, just before Lance's sixth birthday. We waited until Louisa fell asleep sunbathing and then we ran off, straight to the cave, our secret place. Clever little boys we were! We kept torches with us at all times, just in case we got an opportunity to explore our secret hideaway any further – and there it was! Being small and quick we reached the cave ever so easily. We were excited like never before – two young boys discovering this great hall. It was magnificent..."

With this Petroc has to stop for a moment to compose himself. Tears are running down his face, his voice is vibrating. Although I am cold and tired I am trying to comfort him as his suffering is becoming very obvious now.

"We started playing, over there, near the recess, when we heard voices. We were so afraid that we switched our torches off. As the voices drew nearer we needed to hide as fast as we could in the recess, just like you did," Petroc continues, weeping.

"Two people, two voices, one male, one female – they entered the hall as we squeezed ourselves deeper into the rocks. We wanted to cry out loud but we never got the chance. The couple, my mum and his dad, started kissing, undressing, doing things we had never seen before, the echo in here repeating their every word, their groans and screams. We were horrified, did not understand what was going on. Witnessing it was shocking and totally fascinating at the same time. We hid in those rocks until it was over. The couple left. For minutes we were unable to speak. When we got back to the beach I remember holding on to Lance who was just that little bit younger than me, saying: this must be our secret, forever. Promise me to never tell anyone, ever."

"By now Louisa had woken up and was worried about our whereabouts. She eventually found us but not the lovers. Soon after this my parents split up – of course, I was too young to make a connection. Max never left Louisa. She had brought the money into the family, enabled him to go into business, live a comfortable life. My mum must have been upset at the time but children of that age don't get it, do they? Lance and I never discussed the affair again. We agreed not to return to the cave. Our bond was strong but what we had experienced had a profound effect on us. I was haunted by what I had seen throughout my adolescence."

"Maybe that's why I became a difficult teenager. It was all getting too much for my mum so she decided that I should live with my gran while my brother stayed with her. Nobody explained to me why I was being separated from my brother at the time and I became rather rebellious. Luckily my gran encouraged me to learn another instrument. Music was all I was ever interested in. I felt that I could express myself through music, if you know what I mean. From an early age I found refuge in music. I already played the piano so I chose the guitar next and loved it. Gran also realised that I had a good voice and she paid for singing lessons. My music took my mind off all the things I did not understand."

"Lance excelled at sport. He was bright, academically, but his talent for golf took over. Day in, day out, he spent all his time on the golf course. Max made him go to uni, get a degree but Lance decided to become a pro and work in golf. Although we are still good friends we have drifted apart. I don't know why but I think that what he saw that day affected him badly too. He finds it difficult to hold down relationships, make a commitment to women," Petroc explains.

I am astounded how vividly he can remember what happened so many years ago. The young boys' experience has caused deep scars which may never fully heal.

"And when did you turn to God, decide to make this your church, your own?" I ask him carefully.

Fortunately his tears have ceased and he is breathing more regularly now.

"When we formed Monopoly. I had been in a couple of bands before, at college and after. It did not work out. I wanted to write different music, another genre. Recruiting Jamie and Pete was fairly easy but convincing them of my plans for the new band less so. Once I got them hooked they enjoyed the new style – the only problem was that they needed me to write the songs, both the lyrics and the music. In the beginning I felt under pressure. I needed a place to call my own, somewhere where I could be completely by myself, where I could experiment to my heart's content."

"Returning to this cave was tough but I was an adult by then, no longer afraid of the memories, although still haunted. Once I started working here the inspiration just came. The acoustics, the surroundings – it was unreal, absolutely perfect. I was so totally in awe of this place and I felt that God was talking to me, right to the core, bringing out the very best in me. It was here that I became a true Christian, a believer. Whatever happens I will be eternally grateful for the time I was allowed to spend here in the presence of God. This was my spiritual home but now it's over. I, we, shall never return. Since clearing the church out I have come back here every night, waiting for you but you did not appear. Then I decided that it was time to seal my fate, perform the final closure. So I searched for a large rock that would forever cover up the gap, block the entrance, deter from any further visits. It was hard to push that huge specimen of rock into position but I did it. I had no idea that you were in there but then I saw the light, candle light. At first I did not realise it was you. I could not be sure. Perhaps I should have investigated straight away but my troubled mind was full of anger, fear and disappointment. It may have been foolish but I wanted to let the latest intruder stew, knowing that I would find out sooner or later who was in here. This is why I sat in front of the rock in the pouring rain until you pushed the boulder from the inside."

Overcome by emotions Petroc fails to continue. We are rising from the sandy ground together. My arms paining from the earlier effort I wrap them tightly around Petroc's slim, damp body. As we step forward he accidentally kicks his torch. It strikes a piece of sharp rock in the sand and shatters, leaving nothing but eerie-looking white smoke rising from the ground until it sends the former church into complete darkness. I hold Petroc in my arms and kiss him. Through his wet clothing I can feel his heart beat. Our lips find each other so easily. At this moment in time I do not believe that I have ever loved anyone as much as I love Petroc. Here, in this mysterious chamber, God is speaking to us. Finally, I understand what Petroc means, and even I am no longer in doubt about the existence of the Holy Spirit.

"Let's pray, together, and then we must leave, forever," I suggest firmly.

Closing our eyes we kneel down in the sand. Our hands folded we each hold our silent prayers before we get up, trying to adjust to the total darkness around us. Carefully we creep out of the great hall, through the narrow tunnel, along the wet mossy passage until we reach the boulder outside. Together we push the massive rock back in front of the entrance. It has stopped raining, the wind blowing the last dark clouds away as morning is breaking.

THE END